THE PATH
OF
BUCK CROSS

LOUISE RIVEIRO-MITCHELL

Dedication:

In honor of my newest granddaughter Luna Katherine,
I dedicate this story to her.

Chapter 1

The afternoon sun started its journey across the range working its way down the valley to its resting place behind the mountains. On the other side, high on a ridge Kit Taylor sits on her horse enjoying the mystical sight. This was by far Kit's most favorite time of day. There was something magical that happened as the colors of red and orange streamed across the range bathing all in its path with a glow of warmth. Oh, there were others who only saw it as a sunset, but to Kit, it was something more.

Her brothers tended to laugh at her and call her a foolish female, but to her it was magic and if they felt she was just a foolish female, then so be it. She knew what she saw, and she would believe that maybe it was meant for her to believe and not them. It was not easy being the only girl and the youngest child. but Kit was the only daughter of Ben and Alice Taylor. Born Katherine Irene Taylor, named after both grandmothers, she grew up with the name Kit, given her by her father. Four years before her, Eli was born and two years before him the oldest boy Jacob was born. If they were not sure what to do with a baby sister always around, Kit made it known she was not letting anyone tell her she couldn't do it 'cause she was a girl. Nothing was going to keep her down and at the age of five, she was on a horse helping move the cattle.

It was a few years after the war and like all their neighbors, the Taylors were having a hard time making their farm come back again. The crops were destroyed, land was scorched and it would take years to bring it back. The wells were all contaminated and the stock had either run off or were taken by soldiers or looters. It was the chore every day for Ben and the boys to haul large barrels down to the creek and fill them with water just to have water to drink and cook with. The luxury of bathing and clean clothes was often put on hold for a while. Yes, it was safe to say the war had almost destroyed this country of ours. One thing for sure, it was gonna be a long while before the land here in the Shenandoah Valley would be the piece of heaven on earth folks had once called it. Why just seeing it would bring a smile on a body's face. But that was before the war, the war that took that piece of heaven and destroyed it.

Standing in the charred field Ben Taylor held the black dirt in his hands and slowly watched it blow out if his hands. He looked about the farm that his pa built with his own hands, the only reason it was still standing was because it was used as a hospital for the wounded. The barn was long gone along with the stock except for the one horse. On the far end of the farm was the graves of Ben's folks, thankfully they were untouched by all this.

Each night Ben would look at his wife and children knowing there had to be an answer. Some ray of hope to get them through this and to a better life. Two weeks later in a roundabout way it came, while in town to get supplies, Ben heard about land out west. Good land going to families like his, willing to take the trip out there and work on the land for five years and then it would be there's. On the way back home, Ben thought about the idea, and the more he thought about it the more it sounded like the answer he'd been looking for. Free land for the taking and it would be theirs, why it was too good to be true. He arrived back home that afternoon and had to tell Alice the good news.

He knew any decision had to be made in complete agreement, but he really was hoping Alice would be as excited about this as he was. He would point out to her that for the past ten years they have tried to save their home, there just wasn't any use, it was gone, and no amount of praying would ever bring it back. He sat Alice down in the parlor room and took her hand,

"Alice, I know we always said if anything we had to agree on something together, well I'm asking you to listen to me on this."

She tries to get up but he sets her back down, "now Alice, you ain't even heard me yet. Now just set and listen, please."

She looks at him, "alright Ben, I'm listening."

"Well you know we've been praying for an answer to our problem here and in town today I heard that the government is giving out land to people out west." He saw the look in his wife's eyes, "now Alice you know you said you would listen to me."

She nodded and listened to him continue. "Well, I says to myself, free land and good land from what they're saying. Well, I'd be a fool not to grab some of it for my own."

Alice looked at him, "so that's what you said was it?"

"Yes I did.'

She looked at him, "and where is this good land that you want for your own?"

"Well it is a bit west, but we can be there is a few months."

"How far west is this land?"

He sat down now knowing Alice for sure will not agree to this one. "It's in the Oregon territory."

At this point Alice gets off the chair, "Oregon! Dear Lord in heaven, have you gone completely mad Benjamin Taylor?"

"Now Alice, I was thinking of you and the kids. We have been struggling here for six years now and we still…."

She looks at him, she really couldn't be angry at him. "Benjamin, I'm sorry I should not have yelled at you. I know it's been hard and I sit her at times and remember what this valley was like before the war. Oh it really was beautiful Ben wasn't it?"

"That it was Alice that it was."

She looked into his eyes and saw the dreams he had come back to life. "Alright Ben, if you feel that strongly about this we will go to the Oregon territory."

He takes her in his arms and kisses her. "You'll see I promise you Alice, we'll have a farm like this once was."

Alice looked out the window again she remembered what it was how the scent of lavender would softly float into the windows at night and the soft cool breeze that told one the season was changing; those now were just locked in her mind. Memories that would come out a visit every now and then. She looked across and saw the resting place of Ben's folks, they came to this valley and built the house, raised three sons. Lost two in a war that tore this country apart and now their only boy, grown up and leaving them behind. She wondered if they would understand, if they would hold it against Ben, if they would forgive him? She understood why he was doing it and she loved him for it even if no one could.

He looks at her, "I promise you'll never regret this."

She smiles at him.

He looks into her eyes, eyes that were green as moss growing on the side of a tree with tiny flecks of gold in them when the sun hit them just right. "I promise you Alice I'll make it work. We'll have everything we had and no one will ever take it from us." He puts his arms around her and slowly her arms go around his neck as she draws him closer to her.

Suddenly the front door burst open and in run eight-year-old Jacob and six-year-old Eli. "Papa, Papa, did you get anything for us?"

Alice couldn't help but laugh," well Ben did you get anything for the boys?"

Ben smiles as he reaches into his vest pocket and pulls out two peppermint sticks, "seems these two sticks fell into my pocket when I was at Mr. Kroger's store. Do you know who would want them?"

Jacob grabbed them and handed one to his younger brother and started to head back outside when Alice stops them, "don't you have something to say to your pa?"

Eli smiles, "thanks Pa."

Jacob looks at his father, "thanks Pa." Then they both head back out the door."

Alice looks at him, "well Ben, do you have a plan on how we are going to get to this new life?"

He gently takes he hand and walks back into the parlor, sits her down and with great detail explains how the entire family would be going to this land of dreams. He went on to explain that an act of congress set up parcels of land that would be available to families to work on and in five years the land would be theirs.

Alice listened with great interest and it all, sounded very interesting, but how they would get there was still the question Ben didn't answer. "It all sounds very nice Ben and I do share your idea, but how do you plan on getting us there?"

He looked at her and smiled, "by wagon train of course."

She smiled and nodded," and we're to take all our belongings on a wagon some 2,000 miles away from here?"

He looked at her, "well of course we can't take everything Alice."

And so three weeks later, the Taylor family loaded up their wagon and made one last visit to the gravesite. Ben lingered a bit longer saying his goodbyes hoping, somehow, his pa would understand and forgive him for leaving. He slowly turned and walked to Alice waiting by the wagon with Kitt. The boys were on their horses and as he helped Alice up the Kitt he took one last look at the house and climbed up on the wagon and headed down the road. The mikes, the weather, Indians, and nature bonded these souls together for one goal to make it through to the Oregon territory and their dream of a better life.

Chapter 2

Ben sat quietly on his front porch watching the sun set. It's hard to imagine he and the family have been out here twelve years now. Even after all this time the sunsets still mesmerize him as much as the first one he saw. It was this bond he and Kitt had with the sunsets. Why he could just about guarantee she was on that ridge watching the sun do her magic for the day. As he leans back he finds it hard to imagine that Kit is almost a grown woman. Why she was all of three years old when they arrived here and now she's no longer three. He remembered how Alice fretted each time he would put her on a horse, but in spite of it all she ended up being a better rider than her brothers. But now that she was getting older maybe it was time Kit became more of a young lady. Living on the farm all these years and only going into town once a month was no life for a young lady. Why back home there would be parties and socials not to mention gentlemen waiting to ask her to dance. He realized she never has learned to dance, there was so much she needed to learn and time was slipping by so fast. He sat back and thought on it. His Kit dancing, meeting a fine young man and settling down, even having a young'un or two. Lost in his thoughts he didn't notice Alice walk on to the porch.

"Watching the sunset Ben?"

He looks at her and nods. "Somehow I think you and Kit have this bond with the sunsets." He reaches up and takes her hand gently pulling her beside him in the chair. "I was just thinking, it's time Kit got out more."

She looks at him, "Oh?"

"Yes, you see keeping her from the finer things well, she don't even know she's becoming a lady and I want my daughter to be as fine and as any of those other girls in town. She deserves fine clothes and fancy dresses."

"I understand Ben but there isn't really a need for fancy dresses her on the farm."

"Still my little girl will have fancy dresses just like all the others and she'll go to parties and…"

Alice smiles and tries to calm him down, "yes she will have all that, but when the time is right and right now it isn't."

"Well when the time comes I want to make sure our girl is ready."

Alice shakes her head, "Benjamin Taylor, sometimes I wonder what possessed me to marry you?"

He took her hand in his, "You saw the man you wanted to spend the rest of your life with."

"I saw everything I ever wanted and still want in you. That's what I saw."

They both sat back hand and hand and watched the sunset.

On the ridge Kit was just about to turn and head home when she saw someone walking on the trail below. It seemed odd for anyone to be walking this time of day since there clearly was nothing around for miles. Could it be his horse became lame causing him to walk, if that is so, where is his horse? Slowly she made her way down the ridge and rode towards him.

The man stopped when he saw the rider coming toward him. He hadn't noticed the rider was a girl, but then again, the way Kit dressed, no one would ever suspect she was a girl.

As she got closer she slowed to a stop. "Howdy mister, you seem to have a bit of problem?"

He raised his head and looked up at her, "now why would you say that?"

"Well for one thing, ya'll are out here in the middle of nowhere and have no horse. 'Sides it'll be dark soon."

He just notices she's a girl, and a pretty one at that. "Well ma'am, I've walking this road for quite a few days now, ever since my horse came lame a few days back and well, I left her with some fine folks and I started walking."

"You left your horse…"

"Well I couldn't very well leave her on the trail. It just wouldn't be right. Anyway I got my canteen and rifle and gun, besides it's not so bad sleeping out under the stars."

"Well suit yourself." She turns and is about to ride off when he calls out to her, "'cuse me ma'am, not meaning no disrespect or being too formal, but what would you be doing out here at this time of day?"

Kit turns and smiles, "no disrespect taken, you're on Taylor land as far as the eye can see in any direction."

"And I take it you're a Taylor."

"Yes, I'm Kit Taylor, my papa owns this here farm."

The young man looks at her, "Kit?"

She looks back and smiles, "Kit."

He smiles and shakes his head, "Well, Miss Taylor, would be breaking the law if I spend the night on your pa's land?"

"No by now I'm sure my mama would take a hickory switch to my hide if I didn't show proper respect to a stranger and invite you to spend the evening at our home. Meaning no disrespect, but ya'll look like you haven't had a good meal in a while and I'm sure my papa would let you have a horse to get into town at least."

He smiled at her, she really was a right pretty little thing even dressed in boys' clothes. "Well that would be mighty nice of him Miss Taylor."

"It's just Kit. If you like I can give you a ride to the house."

He looked at her, "you want me to ride with you?"

She smiles at him, "you don't mean to tell me you ain't never ridden on the back of a horse before."

"Well of course I have. I just never rode with a gal in the front."

"Well that's the only way I can offer you mister… By the way, I didn't get your name."

"It's Cross, Buck Cross."

"Well Mr. Cross are you ready to get on the back of Powder Keg? I promise I'll be real gentle."

He looks at the horse, then her, "Powder Keg?"

"That's his name." She offers him her hand to help him up and he gets up on the horse. As he puts his arms around her waist there was no mistaken, she was a girl.

"Hold on Mr. Cross, we don't want y'all falling off powder keg."

"I'll have you know Miss. Taylor, I have never…"

Before he could finish Kit gives a gentle kick to the horse and he's off in full gallop forcing Buck to hold on to Kit tighter.

Chapter 3

It was just about dusk when Kit and Buck Cross came riding up the road to the house. It was Alice who noticed Kit had someone behind her. "Wonder who that might be?"

Ben looks up, "don't look like nobody I know."

As she nears closer to them, she smiles and brings the horse to a stop. Swinging her right leg over the saddle horn she gets off the horse, followed by Buck. "Papa, Mama, this here is Mr. Buck Cross. I found him walking along the trail, his horse come up lame a few days back and he's been walking for the past few days.

Ben looks at Buck, "you say your horse came up lame?"

"Yes sir."

"Would ya be inclined to tell me where you left your horse?"

"Yes sir, I left my horse with a man named Hollister. I believe his first name was Matthew."

Ben seemed pleased with that answer. He knew Matt Hollister and could easily have the story checked out. It was Kit who spoke up, "well you see Papa, since Mr. Cross has been on the trail for the past few days I was wondering if you might let him spend the night where he can get a fresh start in the morning."

Ben nods his head, never let it be said that Ben Taylor turned away someone down on his luck. "I think that can be arranged, but before that perhaps Mr. Cross would care to have supper with us? My Alice is a fine cook Mr. Cross."

Buck smiles at Alice then looks back at Ben, "well Mr. Taylor, all I can say is if her cooking is as good as she is pretty I would be honored, sir."

Ben pats him on the back, "good, then it's settled. Come on inside and we'll have some time to relax before supper."

He looks at Kit, "go fetch your brothers, tell them it's supper time."

Kit leaves them and heads to the barn. Ben escorts Buck into the house, through the hall and to the kitchen in the back. Alice looks up and smiles, "Mr. Cross, if you'd like to wash up, there's a pitcher of water and a pan out past that door."

"Thank ya ma'am and please it's just Buck."

She smiles at him, "alright Buck."

He makes his way out the door and to the washroom.

She looks at her husband, "you know Ben, maybe Buck could stay on a few days. After all, if he's down on his luck, he might a place to stay. Just until he can get things in order."

"Alice, we don't know anything about him."

"Well he's been sleeping on the ground for the past two nights. I'm sure he hasn't eaten anything for the same amount of time, he has manners just listen to the way he talks and for one thing he didn't try to steal Powder Keg from Kit."

In the barn Kit informs her brothers supper's ready and that they have company. "Papa told me to come and get you, supper's ready. Oh yea we have company."

As she's about to walk out, her brother Jacob stops her, "who is the company."

"Someone I met in the trail."

Her brother looks at her, "does he have a name?"

"Well of course he has a name, it's Buck Cross."

The name doesn't sound familiar to him and they follow their sister out and walk to the house. Jacob looked at Buck and recognized him.

Buck looks at him and extends his hand, "Hi, I'm Buck Cross."

Jacob takes his hand and shakes it, "Jacob Taylor."

Eli does the same only he doesn't recognize Buck as a federal marshal.

Jacob has seen him last year at Fort Harney when he and Matt Hollister's boys sold some stock to the Army for the Indians on the reservation. Buck was handling the distributing of the beef. It was Jacob who asked the question, "my sister says you've been on foot for the past few days. She says your horse came up lame."

"Yes, I was lucky enough to find Mr. Hollister and he offered to take care of my horse."

"Odd he didn't offer you a horse just to get into town."

"Well to tell you the truth, I didn't realize how far the man lived from town."

Buck really wanted to come clean with the reason for him being here especially now that Jacob recognizes him, but he just couldn't let anyone know why he was here. Most of his story was true and his horse did become lame. It was also true that Hollister offered to tend to the animal until she healed. But it was Hollister who had written to Washington about the unrest out here. Seems someone has been supplying the Indians with rifles, repeaters to be exact and small parties have been attacking the small farms in the area, so far all they have done was to steal some stock, but before it turns bad and settlers' lives are at risk someone needs to find out who is doing it. Buck was sent since he was familiar with the Paiute tribe and being part Kiowa himself, he was the perfect choice for the assignment. Though he had no plan on how to undertake this task it seemed the spirits smiled upon him and put him into the path of the lovely Kit Taylor.

According to Hollister's letter, the problem started early in May, the Paiutes had suffered a heavy winter and the land given them by Washington was being used by local settlers to graze their stock. Someone got the braves all worked up, handed them rifles and the feud started. For now it was only a few cattle that were taken from the farms, but if it continued there could be a real Indian war on their hands and that will mean a lot if killing on both sides. Buck's job was to find who is getting the guns to the Indians and why.

Ben was already sitting at the table when Buck and the others came to sit down. Ben looked up and noticed Buck and the boys. "Ah good, you've met my boys. Come sit down, don't be shy."

Kit goes to sit and Buck holds the chair for her. She looks at him, "I wasn't gonna fall."

Alice smiles, "no dear, it's customary for a gentleman to hold the chair for a lady." As Alice begins to sit, Buck holds the chair for her also. She smiles at him, "thank you Mr. Cross."

"You're welcome ma'am." He sits himself on the side of Kit as the boys are seated on the other side of the table. Kit passes him the platter of meat, he smiles and passes it to Alice.

Ben looks at Buck, "don't be shy son eat up, my Alice will be offended if ya'll don't eat her food."

"Ben, stop bothering the boy, there's plenty more he can always get it later." Alice smiles at him, "don't you get upset with Ben, Mr. Cross, sometimes he forgets his manners."

"I understand ma'am, no need to worry."

She looks at him, the boy had the manners of a gentleman and yet here he was out here where there are so few of them. There was something different about him though that she couldn't be sure. Whatever it was he was definitely not just some cowboy.

He smiled as he saw her looking at him, "I can honestly say ma'am, it's been a long time since I had such a fine meal. I thank you and Ben for the honor of dining with you. If there's anything I can do for you, please don't hesitate to ask."

She smiled at him, "well that is kind of you Mr. Cross, there is something I would like, there seems to be a storm coming and I wouldn't feel right with you out in bad weather. Could I possibly ask you to stay the night here and leave in the morning?"

Buck looks at Ben who nods in agreement then back to Alice, "if it makes you happy ma'am, you have your wish."

"Oh wonderful, Kit make up the spare room down the hall for Mr…" She looks at Buck," You know I really feel silly calling you Mr. Cross, may I call you Buck?"

Buck smiles at her, "if you'd like ma'am."

The meal ended with Ben taking Buck with him into his office. It wasn't much of an office, just a small room with a desk and a few chairs. Ben used it for doing the books on the farm and an occasional meeting of fellow neighbors when something would come up. He led Buck in and closed the door. "Sit down my boy, any chair is fine. Would you care for a drink?"

"No thank you sir."

Ben sits down behind his desk, "well I know you told us about how you got here and Matt Hollister has your lame horse, but can you tell me how you know my son Jacob? Now don't be denying it. I saw the look you gave each other when he came in from the barn. You'd better be telling me now for I'll surely find out."

Buck looked at him. He knew he had to tell him it was only right. "Alright Ben, I feel I should tell you the truth. First off, the truth is my horse did go lame and Mr. Hollister did offer to care for her. As for knowing your son, I saw him at Fort Kearney last year when I was overseeing the buying of stock for the Paiute's. I really didn't think he'd remember me.

Now the reason I'm here is I was asked by the Army to answer a letter they got from Matt Hollister. The letter stated that some farmers have been using land given to the Paiutes to graze their cattle. Well, the Indians felt that the Army gave them the steers along with the land. Seems there was a big ta do and well, the farmers got up in arms calling the Indians cattle rustlers. Well push comes to shove and somebody decided to supply the Paiutes with rifles, repeaters. I'm here to find out who, before things get out of hand and we have an Indian war with both sides having casualties."

Ben looks at hm, "so you're an…"

"I'm a United States Federal Marshal Ben."

Ben leans back in his chair, "I see and you just happened to be on the road when Kit saw you."

"Yes sir. I ask you to keep this in confidence sir."

Ben looks at him, "Yes, yes of course. Tell me son, would it be a better idea if you had a reason to be here in the part of the country? I mean a cover?"

"Sir?"

Ben gets up from his chair, "now here you are with no horse, no saddle, not even a job plus you are clearly educated for this neck of the woods. My boy, you stick out like a sore thumb."

Buck looks at him as Ben continues, "tell you what I'm gonna do for you. I'm gonna offer you a job here on the circle T. You will have all the time you want to check out any place on the farm no one will ask questions. Also as one of my hands none of the neighbors will question you if you just happen to wander on their lands. How does that sound?"

Buck looks at the man and smiles, "That sounds pretty good Ben, I thank you for the help."

"Good I'll go to the neighbors in the morning and tell them I've hired a new hand."

In the spare room Kit was busy getting the sheets on the bed and fluffing the pillows, when her mother walks in. "Well it certainly will feel a lot better than the ground under him tonight."

"Oh Mama, that was so nice of you to offer him to stay the night, it does look there's gonna be a storm soon. I would hate to think of anyone caught out in it."

Alice looks at her, "anyone or just one?"

"Mama!"

Alice just smiles, it's not that she didn't notice the looks Kit was giving Buck at supper only Buck didn't seem to notice them. Seems there was something else on his mind. "Well when you're done, you better head up to bed also."

"Yes Mama."

The loud clap of thunder startled Buck from his sleep and he jumped up in bed. The rain outside beat down on the roof sounding as if it would break through.

He heard a gentle tapping on his door. "Mr. Cross, are you awake?" It was Kit. Slowly in the dark he made his way to the door and gently opened it. There stood Kit with the soft glow of the candlelight on her face. "I just wanted to make sure you were alright? I heard a loud crash and..."

"It's just the thunder. It woke me up too."

Feeling a bit foolish she starts to turn and head back to the stairs, when Buck stops her, "ya know if thunder bothers you I'd be happy to sit with you until the storm blows over."

She turns to him, "that's mighty kind of you Mr. Cross, but I've taken up enough of your time."

"Don't be silly and it's no trouble after all if I hadn't run into you I'd be out there in that rain right now. So what do you say?" He looked at her and smiled, "and I think you can call me Buck, after all I'll be working for your pa now." He takes her hand and they walk into the kitchen.

Kit sets the lamp on the table and prepares to make some coffee. "I'm really sorry for waking you up and…"

"I told you it's alright." He walks over and looks out the window, "that rain is really coming down hard."

Kit moved closer just as she a flash of lightning came down right by the window on the outside and Kit grabbed Buck's arm. She instantly removed her hand, but not before Buck took her hand and held it.

"It's okay Kit, it's only lightning, you're safe here."

"I'm sorry it came so sudden I wasn't expecting…"

He gently squeezed her hand and smiled, "like I said, it can't hurt you in here."

She looked at him, "how can you be so sure?"

He smiles at her, "there's a saying among my people that the Great Spirit sends light down from the sky to lead us to our next path that we are to follow."

She questions him, "your people?"

"Yes, my mother was the daughter of a Kiowa chief. My father was a trapper. He was up in the mountains when an early winter storm hit and the snow began to block all the passages. He made his way half way down only to realize he was totally lost. My grandfather's braves found him covered with snow and took him back to their village. Many thought he was dead, but my grandmother knew different. The snow covered him and protected him from the freezing temperature and keeping any body heat he had in him close to his body. It took many weeks for him to recover from the ordeal. Both my mother and grandmother nursed him until he was able to move around on his own. It soon came time for him to leave, once again the pass was clear and the snow was gone. He had become very fond of my mother during this time and he knew he would be sorry to leave her.

They were walking outside of the village when a storm came from nowhere. Storms like that was not normal that time of year. There was the rumble of thunder and then a bolt of light came down before them and caused the tree directly in front of them to come crashing down blocking their path. It was the same path my father would take to get back to his people.

When they got back to the village my grandfather told him it was a sign from the Great Spirit. It was the sign he was to stay with them."

Kit looked at him and began to smile, "did he stay? I mean…"

He stayed for the rest of his days with my mother's people. They married and had six children. Three girls and three boys. My father worked for the Army in his younger days as a surveyor and taught me and my brothers not only his language, but much of the history as the white men called it. My brothers chose to follow the ways of my mother's people. I chose to go down the mountain to see what life was like with my father's people."

"And you stayed."

He looked at her, "yes I stayed." He smiled at her.

"Your sisters and brothers?"

"My sisters married, my brothers Spotted Horse and Lone Wolf were killed in battle. It happened before I left. It's one of the reasons my mother agreed to let me go. She said she wanted to make sure one of her son's would stay alive.

Kit put her head down, "I'm sorry. I didn't mean to..."

He took her hand in his, "it's been long time since I spoke of them. Thank you for giving me that moment to remember them."

She looked up at him, "and what about you? Do you want to go back to your people? I'm sorry it was wrong of me to ask that question."

He looked deep into her eyes, "Miss Taylor, you can ask me that question again when my work here is done. I promise you, I will give you my answer then."

Suddenly the rain stopped, the thunder and lightning ceased and the darkness was beginning to show patches of light. They had spoken through the storm and soon the morning would be upon them.

Kit got up from the chair, "I'd better get dressed and start breakfast."

She headed up the stairs and Buck blew out the lamps and headed to his room. There in his room he thought about his family. It's been many years since he had seen them. Too many years had passed for him to go back again. He also realized this young girl had somehow found a memory of long ago and opened up more about him, more than anyone else could. In the course of the storm he found that maybe his path was about to change yet again. Maybe this young girl named Kit would show him the way.

Chapter 4

It was sunup when riders came up to the Taylor farm. Local neighbors of Ben's, Amos Hunter, Sam Butler, Bill Franks. All like Ben had come out here years back and started a new life. A life that now was being threatened by these savages as they were called.

As Ben heard them ride up he went out to greet them. "Morning Amos, Sam, Bill what brings you out here this time of the morning?"

It was Amos who started the conversation, "it's those savages Ben! They're at it again. Only this time they've gone too far."

"Savages?"

"They came down from the hills early last night before the storm. They raided the Henderson farm. John and Helen tried to hold them off, but there were just too many of them. Little Patricia rode out to get help, but we got there too late, they were both dead. You know what that means Ben, they broke the treaty. This means they are on the war path. We need to get the Army here and put a stop to this before it's too late. We need to destroy these savages before they destroy us."

Ben looked at them, he knew these men, he also knew the Henderson's. All were peace loving, there was no need for this raid.

He thought of Buck and how he should keep his promise to him on his identity, but he still should know what is happening. "I'll be right back boys. Please get off your horses, and sit down." When he gets back inside he sees Alice heading toward the door.

"What's wrong Ben?"

"Where's Buck? I need to talk to him. It's important."

"He's in the kitchen. Ben what's wrong?"

He places his hands on her shoulders, "I'll tell you in a while, but I need to speak to Buck right now." He heads to the kitchen where Buck is sitting with Jacob, Eli, and Kit.

It's Kit who greets him, "Papa, what's wrong?"

He doesn't answer her, but looks straight at Buck," I need to speak with you alone son. Right now!"

Buck looks at him, "is it about the men outside?"

"I really need to talk to you alone about this Buck."

Jacob gets up and looks at the others, "come on guys, we're not wanted here."

Ben didn't like his tone of voice and answered him, "this is nothing that concerns you."

"He answers him," oh but it concerns Buck. Since when did he become more important than your children?"

It was Kit who came to Buck's defense, "Jacob, maybe it has nothing to do with us. Papa would tell us if it did."

Jacob looks at his sister, "well lookie here, little sister sticks up for the stranger. Is our little sister sweet on the stranger? Tell me Kit, do you know he's a half breed?"

Kit lifts her hand and smacks his face hard enough to not only hear the impact, but to make Jacob fall back slightly. "Now you apologize Jacob Taylor, or I'll hit you again and this time you will fall."

Jacob looks at his sister, never had she struck him, "you realize he is a half breed, Pa tell her she'll believe you."

Ben looks at his son, "you have no right to say anything about anyone as long as they're a guest in my home. And as long as he is in our home, we all will treat him with respect. Do I make myself clear?" He looks at Buck, "will you be kind enough to join me in my office son?"

Buck nods and gets up and heads for the office door.

Ben looks at his sons, "I will deal with both of you later." With that he walks into the door with Buck.

Inside the office Ben tells Buck what happened with the Henderson's.

Buck looks at him," well I'm afraid I'm gonna have to tell these men out there who I really am, before they take the law in their own hands."

"I wouldn't do that son, you see if they find out what you are, they will string you up from the nearest tree."

"But Ben…"

"Look son, I don't know you but more than a day, but if ya'll want to be around to see more sunrises, I suggest you follow my story out there. You are Buck Cross, a friend of my brother in law who's on his way to California. Think you can do that.?"

Buck shakes his head, "if that's what you want."

Ben smiles, "for now we need to do it my way son." He gets up and heads to the door and they both head out of the office.

As they reached the front door Ben sees Alice has gotten all three men off their horses and sitting on the porch having coffee. As Ben and Buck come out to the porch Alice turns and smiles, "well here you two are. I was telling the boys we have a new hand working here for a while."

Ben nods, "Amis, Sam, Bill this is …"

Before he could finish his sentence, Buck extends his hand Amos, "Buckley Edward Cross sir, but everyone calls me Buck."

Amos nods and shakes his hand. "Pleased to meet you son."

Ben smiles, "Buck here is a friend of my brother in law who's on his way to California."

Sam shakes the boy's hand and smiles, "wanna get rich panning for gold? Let me tell ya staying here and getting a nice spread is a better deal."

Ben smiles, "I tried to tell him but you know these young folk, they seem to think that California has streets filled with gold dust."

All three men laughed at that. Alice put her hand in Buck's and squeezes it, "now you men stop that. I think of Buck has a dream to go to California. He should, after all, didn't we all have our dreams to come out here?"

They thought for moment and started to nod and Alice felt she had made her point. She lets go of Buck's hand and gets up. "Well if you'll will excuse me, I do have work to do."

They all get up as she heads back in the house. Amos waits for her to get back in the house before he turns to Ben, "so Ben, what do we do about the Indians?"

He looks down then after a few moments he looks up again. "Well I've thought about it, even spoke to Buck about it…"

Bill looks at him, "spoke to him? What does an easterner know about savages?"

Buck steps closer, "well sir, for one, I spent my early years along the Canadian border. My father was a fur trapper when I was younger, I would go with him. We got to know the tribes along the river, even became friendly with some of them. Now Ben told me about the raid and there's only one thing you can do."

"And what's that boy?"

"There is two ways to go on this, you can bring the Army in which could possibly start an Indian war or you can get your cows off their land."

"Get your cows off... sonny they don't even use the land."

Buck looks at him, "be that as it is, but they were given that land by the government and your cows are trespassing."

Bill looks at him, "trespassing, why they don't understand the word."

Buck looks at him, "oh they understand the word very well Mr. Franks, it was the white man who taught him the word. Taught him that they could not trespass on their land, but the white man could do it to theirs"

Amos looked at Buck, "you seem to know quite a bit about the Indian yung fella. Quite a bit for an easterner."

"Like I said my pa was a trapper, he took me with him in the mountains since I could walk. I got to know the ways and customs of the tribes."

Sam looks at him, "and you figure that to move our stock will stop the raids?"

"I would rather see that than a Paiute nation coming down on all of us."

Bill gets up and mounts his horse, "I'm still going to talk to the Army. They're here to protect us from these thieving red skins and they will stop them. By God, if the try to get my herd, I'll shoot every last in of them."

Buck looks at him, "that would be wrong Mr. Franks, if they are on their land, they are in the law. To go on their land and get your cows, you would be trespassing."

He looks at Buck, "well looks like we got us an Indian lover here. I never thought you would side with them red skins Ben and now to have one as a guest…. Sure don't beat all." He gets on his horse and starts to ride out.

Ben looks at Sam and Amos, "well do you two both feel the same way."

Sam looks at him, "we've been friends for a long time Ben, but you have admitted we need to feed our stock and since the land is there…"

Buck steps in, "what if there is compromise, what if you all graze your stock on the lands you have, put them all together as long as they're branded, you have no problem."

Ben looks at them, "this way there is no reason for the raids and we still have our cattle fed. It could work. What do you say Amos, Sam?"

Amos thought about it for a moment, "I'm not saying yes or no Ben. I will need time to think on it. Maybe a day or two, then I will get back to you." With that he gets up along with Sam and they mount their horses and ride out.

Ben looks at Buck, "well son you did your best."

"I just hope it was good enough." They went inside the house when Buck looks at Ben.

"Well Ben, I guess I'd best be moving on. I do appreciate your kindness and all, but I really have to get to Major Marcus before Bill Franks does and blows this all out if proportion and we have an Indian war on our hands."

"Can't you stay a few more days? Maybe Sam and Amos will see what you suggested will work?"

"I'd like to, but I have to get back to the fort."

"I'll saddle up a horse for ya at least, can't see ya walking to town."

"Thanks Ben," He heads toward the spare room to pack his few things and be on his way. He passes Alice in the kitchen," is everything alright Buck?"

"I hope so ma'am. "With that, he heads into the room. A few moments later he comes out and Alice sees he has his belongings with him.

"Leaving us Buck?"

"Well it looks that way ma'am. I want to thank you for everything …."

She stops him, "oh stop, all I did was gave you a hot meal and a place to sleep that was warm and dry."

He took her hands in his and smiled at her, "no ma'am you gave me kindness and made me for that short of a time part of your family and that's something I will not forget." Gently he kissed her hand and walked away.

As he steps on to the porch where Ben has a horse waiting. Ben looks at Buck and shakes his hand, "come back to us soon son."

"I'll try sir." He mounts the horse and rides out.

Upstairs from her bedroom window Kit sees him ride off. "No. no he can't go." She quickly gets on her boots and runs down the stairs as her father comes in the door. "Papa, papa, where did Buck go?"

"Why he's gone. Something came up he had to leave."

"He can't, I promised to show him…" She looked at her brother," did you make him leave?"

Jacob looked at her, "no. What's wrong with you?"

She looked at her father, "Papa I've got to …"

He puts his hands on her shoulders, "what's wrong with you girl?"

"I've got to go Papa."

"You knew he would be going. He had business to attend to and …."

She looked at them all, "you all sent him away. You said it yourself, you don't want his kind around. The way you speak about people like him, like they have a disease that one could catch by speaking to them. You all came out here for a new life, but don't offer the same to others. It's wrong, you're all wrong." She ran out if the house and toward the barn. She still could catch up to him if she hurried. She saddles Powder Keg and rides out before Ben can stop her.

Buck slowly makes his way on the trail when he realizes maybe the Army is not the answer. Maybe a compromise with the Paiutes would be the solution. He turns to the left and crosses onto Indian land.

Not far behind him is Kit trying to catch up to him. As she sees him not more than a few yards ahead she calls out his name and gallops toward him. "Buck! Hey Buck hold up a minute."

He slows down and allows her to catch up to him. When she's finally close to him he looks at her, "can you keep it down? You'll have the whole Paiute nation on us with your yelling."

She really didn't mean to get him upset, she just wanted him to stop. "I'm sorry I only wanted to see you before you left."

"Well you've seen me, now you can back to the farm."

She looks at him, "why are you being so mean? I didn't do anything to you. I thought you cared…"

He looked at her, how could he tell her how he really felt. All he knew is he had to send her back home and now. "Well I don't care, so go back home and leave me alone." He was about to turn her horse around when a party of braves came upon them. A small hunting party about eight, but enough to overpower him if they had to. They took the reins of both his and Kit's horses and began to lead them to their camp.

As they rode side by side Buck never took his eyes off Kit. There she sat in the saddle just looking straight ahead. He would never forgive himself if anything ever happened to her. Though she never looked his way, she felt his eyes on her.

As they arrived at a small camp, both were taken down from their horses and taken into a nearby teepee. One of the braves tied their hands and then tied them together back to back so they couldn't face each other. When that was done the brave left.

It was Buck who spoke first, "Kit, Kit."

She didn't respond.

"Kit, I know you can hear me, answer me!" As he continued to talk he tried to free his hands from the rawhide ties he continued to talk to her. "Now I know you're scared and I understand that you have to remain calm. Do not show any fear Kit. Do you understand what I'm saying? Kit, if you don't want to talk to me just nod yes, you understood what I said."

Suddenly in a voice barely above a whisper he heard her say, "you don't want me around. You said you didn't care about me."

Her words seemed to cut into him like a knife. "I'm sorry Kit. I only wanted…"

She spoke louder now and angrier, "You don't want me around. I'm sorry I even followed you. I'm sorry I even met you on the trail and took you home." Her sobs began again.

"Kit you don't understand. I didn't want you to get hurt."

She lashed out at him, "Just leave me alone. I don't ever want to talk to you again."

Silently they sat as Buck tried to loosen the rawhide ties on his hands. Kit just kept her head down and her eyes closed praying for someone to come and rescue her. Meanwhile, back at the Taylor farm, Ben sits on his front porch waiting to see any sign of his daughter returning.

Alice comes out to the porch and sits beside him, taking his hand in hers she looks at him, "you know you had to let her go Ben. She's not a child anymore. Good or bad, she has to learn these lessons in life. Our job now is to be there for her if she needs us."

Ben looks at her, "let her go? Woman have you lost your mind? She's only known this boy a day!"

Alice looked at him, "and these words from a boy who told my father, sir I will marry your daughter. And that was during supper the first day we met."

"That was a different time Alice."

"Really Ben, how so, is there something about this boy I don't know about?"

Ben looks at her, "well for one he's…"

She gives him a stern look, "Benjamin Thomas Taylor, don't you dare say what I think you're about to say."

"I was only going to point out he was part…"

"There ya go. He part nothing, he's a fine gentleman and has conducted himself in my presence as fine a gentleman as any of you so called good Christian folk. As for your daughter, she knows far more than you and your sons give her credit for."

Chapter 5

Back at the Indian camp, with a slight tug, Buck's hands are free. Quickly he unties his ankles and begins to untie Kit's hands. Sleepily Kit once free begins to untie her ankles. He slowly lifts her up and rubs her hands to get circulation back in them. Suddenly the flap of the teepee moves and one of the native women walks in. Buck quickly takes Kit in his arms and passionately kisses her. Almost as if on cue Kit's arms go around Bucks neck and draws him in closer to her body. The native woman looks, smiles, then cast her eyes down and slowly makes her way out of the teepee.

At that moment Kit didn't care who saw them, she was content to stay in Buck's arms forever. Suddenly the flap again pulled up and a brave walks in, he sees them and pulls them apart. He knocks Buck to the ground and makes a grab for Kit when Buck grabs him from behind and stabs him. The brave falls to the floor of the teepee dead. Buck quickly grabs Kit and they slip out and behind the teepee and into the forest of trees.

Kit stumbles and Buck picks her up. "We've got to the far side. We'll be safe until dark, then we can head back to the farm."

She gets up and once again they start moving. The cries of the Indians can be heard in the distance as the others found the dead one in the teepee. They still have a lead and no one saw them leave the teepee. As they approach the clearing, Buck knew once passed, it they would be safe.

As Kit jumped over the log she is surrounded by a forest of trees. Buck follows her and as the sound of the braves come closer, Buck helps Kit crawl under a hollow log and follows her in until the sound of the braves fades into the forest.

It seemed the braves felt that Buck and Kit had gone further into the forest which is what Buck had hoped they would do. Quietly they made their way south in the dark with only the light of the moon to guide them. They had been walking for a while and Kit was beginning to get tired.

Buck sees a large rock up ahead and helps her sit on it to rest. There was still a bit more to get through to be off Indian land, but they had to keep going while it was still dark. He looked at Kit with the moonlight beaming off her hair, it gave it an angelic glow. She was so beautiful, he remembered how she felt in his arms and the warmth she set inside of him. He had to keep his mind on getting them to safety. "I'm sorry I don't have any water to offer you. I can offer you a drink when we get closer to the stream."

She looked up at him, "It's alright." She looked across the rows of trees knowing that once across those trees they would be off Indian land and safe. "Buck, I'm really sorry I caused all this trouble. I... you wouldn't be in all this trouble. I really should have stayed back at home."

He puts his finger to her lips, "Back there you told me you thought I didn't care. I didn't say anything, then, but the truth is Kit, I do care for you. I would do anything to keep you from this. When I kissed you back there, I didn't want to let you go. I wanted to keep you safe in my arms and hold you forever."

She looked at him, "you care for me?"

He takes her hand in his, "more than anyone or anything else in this world. All I want is to get you home safe."

She puts her arms around his neck and he draws her closer to him. "Kit Taylor, I want to spend the rest of my life with you."

Chapter 6

Back at the Taylor farm, Ben sits on the front porch. He just wanted to see Kit ride up the trail to him.

Alice came out and looked at her husband. She too was worried, but she also felt Kit had caught up with Buck and they were safe. "She's fine Ben, trust me, I know she's with Buck and he would not let any harm come to her."

Ben looks at his wife, "I hope you are right."

She sits down beside him and pats his arm, "Come on inside, breakfast is ready."

Buck and Kit reached the clearing and were no longer on Indian land. Slowly they make their way to the clearing and he sits her under a tree and sits beside her.

She looks up at him as he puts his jacket around her to keep warm. "This is the best I can offer you for now Kit. I can get a fire started, but I don't want to get the attention of the Indians."

"It's alright I'll be fine."

He wraps his arms around her and holds her close and she places her head on his chest and starts to nod off. "I'll get you home Kit, I promise."

She smiles and snuggles closer to him, "I am home here with you." They sat together for quite a while, Kit sleeping comfortably with Buck's arms around her. He would keep her like this with him forever, if he could, but the sun was coming up and he knew her folks would be worried about her.

Suddenly she begins to stir and she slowly opens her eyes. Buck looks down at her," I've been waiting for you to get up sleepy head." He leans down and kisses her gently. She smiles at him and kisses him back.

"I had the strangest dream."

"Strange?"

"Yes, we were at an Indian camp and…"

He started to smile, "that was no dream, we were at an Indian camp. They were trailing us until we came on the stretch of land. Now all that's left to do is to take you home."

She looked at him, "you mean we walked through that whole forest and…"

"and I let you sleep, you were too tired to go on."

She looked at him, "and I slept…"

He smiled, "and I watched you."

She lifted her arms up around his neck and kissed him.

His arms went around her and lifted her up but then places her back down, "as much as I'd like to continue this, we should be heading on to get to the house before your pa has the Army out after us."

She gives him a disappointed look and he smiles at her, "we'll pick this up at another time."

"Oh you can be sure of that Mr. Cross." She hands him back his jacket as they start to make their way home.

At Fort Kearney, Bill Franks had given his account of the Paiutes raid on the Henderson's farm and the killing of both John and Helen Henderson. Major Evan Sanders looks up from the report on his desk, "now Mr. Franks you stated here in this report that a band of Paiutes ventured off their land and raided the Henderson farm killing both mister and misses Henderson." The major looks at him, "now it says here not only did they kill the Henderson's, but they stole their whole head of cattle too."

Bill looks at the major, "yes sir, their daughter who was sent by her father to get help told us about the raid. But when we got there, it was too late."

The major gets up from his chair and walks to the side of the desk and points to a map on the wall. "Now can you tell me Mr. Franks where is the Henderson farm?"

Bill walks over to the map and points to an area. "Right about there sir. We're all basically around the same area."

The major looks at him," I see and you all graze your cattle on these parcels of land."

"Yes sir."

"And you are sure there was no reason for the Paiute to come on your lands in this case, no reason for the Paiute to come on the Henderson land, steal his cattle and kill him and his wife. Am I correct on this Mr. Franks?"

Frank looks at him and answers, "Yes sir, no reason at all. That's why I've come here Major, to ask for protection. There's no telling when these savages will come and attack again."

The major moves back to his chair and sits down. He looks up at Bill, "now Mr. Franks, you and the other ranchers know your land boundaries, correct?"

Bill looks at him, "boundaries sir?"

"Yes, boundaries where your land ends and the Indian lands start."

"Oh yes sir."

"Now at any time could any of the cattle on your ranch or any of your neighbors' ranches wander on to the Indian lands?" He looks at Frank. "Now think very hard Mr. Franks on your answer." He waited a few moments and Bill answered," well sir, it's all open range …"

The major stops him, "and there is a good chance a few cows may have strayed onto Indian land. Am I correct?"

"Yes sir, a few had strayed on to that land."

The major opens his desk drawer and takes out a letter that was addressed to him dated a month ago.

"What I have here Mr. Franks is a letter from one of your fellow ranchers. One Amos Hunter. He states in his letter he wanted to bring to my attention the fact the land given to the Paiute tribe by the United States government was in fact being used by the ranchers to graze their cattle on. He looked at Bill, "now I tell you Mr. Franks, using their land to graze your cattle is not only trespassing, but against the law."

"But Major sir, they don't even use the land. They don't deserve it."

The major looked at him and got up from his chair," They don't deserve it? Mister, you do understand the land was theirs first! It never ceases to amaze me how fine upstanding God-fearing folks tend to look the other way at one who has a different color or way of life than theirs. All you Psalm singing, Bible preaching folk forget the words in that book you keep leaning on in times of stress. You know the one that has a young man who says to love your fellow man? Now I'm gonna say this only once. I will look into these charges you have brought to my attention and when the marshal comes back with his report, I will make my decision on what action to take. That is all."

Bill looks at him, "But major…"

"I said that is all Mr. Franks."

It was late afternoon when Kit and Buck reached the outskirts of the Taylor farm. It was the same spot she had first seen Buck. He looked at her. "Well it won't be long Kit, you'll be home before you know it."

There was a sadness to her face, "yes, I'll be home."

"What's the matter?"

"I'll be home and you'll be going back to where ever you came from and…"

He stops her and puts his hands on her shoulders, "hey no matter what, I'm holding you to that promise you made back there in the forest. Don't think I'm gonna walk away and never see you again. I meant what I said. I love you Kit."

She looked at him, "but before we were captured you were leaving, that's why I came after you. I wanted to say goodbye."

He takes her in his arms and holds her close. "I don't want you to think I would never come back to you ever."

She looked at the sky and the sun was about to make its magic like it did every day. She looked at Buck, "it's almost time for the magic."

"Magic?"

"Yes, you see ever since I can remember, I've watched the sun pass across this valley and behind the mountains. If you like you can watch it here with me. Do you like sunsets Mr. Cross?"

"Well that depends Miss Taylor."

"Oh and what would that be?"

He gently places his arm around her shoulder, "well I might be tempted to if I had a pretty gal to watch it with."

"Well maybe you will someday." She makes her way toward a slight incline and sits down and watches the sunset.

Buck comes up beside her and sits down. "You mind if I sit beside you Miss Taylor?"

"Course not Mr. Cross..." Suddenly she stopped as she sees the sun begin to move.

Buck looks at her face, it had a glow about it. A natural beauty, "you know Miss Taylor, sunsets like this one is magical."

She turns and looks at him, "do you really think it is?"

He moved closer to her, "Yes I do." He points to the colors streaming across the valley, "you see there, that's true magic. It's the earth and sky meeting together at the end of the day."

She looks at him all wide eyed like a child, "do you believe that too?"

He smiles, her expression was as innocent as a child's, "yes I do, always have."

She turns to him, "what else do you believe in Buck?"

He smiled when he realized she called him Buck as he continued. "Well I believe that sunsets are special when you share them with someone, someone special."

"Really?"

"Yes, why if it's not shared with someone, and I mean someone special to you, how can you feel the magic?" He gently puts his arm around her waist and draws him closer to him. "Do you remember the first time you saw me? It was right after you saw the sunset?"

Suddenly in the far distance, Buck sees smoke, trying not to alarm Kit, he changes the subject. "I think it's time we head toward the house. 'Spect your ma and pa will be waiting there for ya."

Kit looks at him a bit confused at his sudden change of mood. He helps her up and hastily down the hill as she tries to keep up with his long strides. "Buck can you slow down a bit? I mean no one is after us."

He looks at her, "I know, but I don't want your ma to worry too much. And I don't want to get on your pa's bad side."

As they walk at a normal gait, she looks at him, "I really don't think you could ever get on pa's bad side. I swear he took to you like you were a long-lost son,"

Buck looked at her and smiles, "that's good to hear 'cause I like him a lot."

Back at the Taylor farm, Ben also sees the smoke, one thing he knew for sure, it wasn't no brush fire. "Alice, Alice! Get my gun!"

Alice came running out of the house with her husband's rifle, not knowing what to expect. "What's wrong Ben?"

Ben points, "the north ridge, can you see it woman?"

Her gaze was distracted as she sees Buck and Kit coming up the trail. "Kit, oh my Lord, it's Kit." She rushes down the porch steps and runs to greet them. The two women embrace as Ben makes his way down the steps. Alice looks at her daughter, "Oh Kit we were so worried about you and if you were alright."

Kit tries to control her mother, "yes Ma, I'm fine, Mr. Cross took very good care of me."

Alice looks at Buck and touches his arm, "thank you. Words cannot express my gratitude for taking care of Katherine."

"It was an honor ma'am." She looks deep into his eyes and sees his gaze is on Kit. "Oh my, listen to me talking out here when you two must be exhausted. Come on, let's get you both up to the house and get cleaned up." She takes Kit's arm and they walk up to the house.

Ben is at the steps when he looks at Buck, it's Alice who speaks to him, "Ben, I told the children they need to get cleaned up and get some rest."

Buck looks at Ben, "with all due respect Mr. Taylor, I really should be heading back out."

"Alice take Kit inside. I'll help Buck with what he needs."

"But Ben the boy has been…"

Ben looks at her, "merciful Lord woman, I said get Kit in the house and tend to her."

Alice takes Kit in the house as Ben and Buck head toward the barn. Once out of hearing by the women, Ben looks to Buck, "I spotted the smoke not long before the sunset."

"I saw it too, I decided to get Kit home as fast as I could so she would be safe."

"I appreciate that son. One day you will tell me where you and my daughter were a whole day and night and return with no horses."

He looked at Ben, "let me tell you, nothing happened. After she caught up with me, we were captured by a Paiute hunting party. They took us to their camp. I managed to get us to escape and we wandered through the night to get back here."

Ben looked at him, "a hunting party you say?"

"Yes sir. And that smoke over on that ridge? I'm gonna go see what it is."

Ben looked at him, "you be careful son, I have a feeling that gal of mine is not gonna like it if she knows you've gone off without her again."

"Well I'm gonna try to get to the Paiute village of Running Fox, maybe I can try to see if there is some way this can all be stopped before the Army is called in. There's a lot of blue coats who still have bad feelings on what happened to Custer." Buck heads out of the barn and down the road.

Slowly Ben makes his way back into the house. He walks in to find Kit changed and ready to go out again, "And where do you think you're going?"

She looked at him, "why I'm gonna go with Buck."

He put his hand on her shoulders and directs her to the chair, "you're staying right here young lady. One trip through the forest is quite enough."

She looks at him, "but Papa, you don't understand, we…"

"I understand all too well. You may find it an adventure, but getting captured by a Paiute hunting party and being held as a captive is not a way to spend a night. He's better off alone Kit, he can't stop to worry about your safety."

"But Papa…"

Ben looks at her, "Now don't you be worrying, the boy will be back, on that you can be sure of."

Kit gets up and runs up the stairs to her room and slams the door.

Alice walks over to her husband, "did you have to be so cruel to her Ben?"

"Cruel, is that what I was? Let me tell you my dear woman, that boy has just spent the past 24 hours making sure that daughter of ours was safe and no harm would come to her. Now he didn't have to tell me the whole story of what happened and I'm sure he would lay down his own life for that hot-headed female upstairs, but truth be known, he was honest and he's in love with her."

Alice looked at him, "did he tell you that?"

Ben smiled, "he didn't have to, the look on his face told it all. He's in love with that girl and if my hunch is right, she's fond of him also."

Alice smiles at him, "Ben Taylor, it took you that long to realize that? I saw it in her eyes the first day he came here."

Ben looks at his wife, "well I guess I'd better go up and apologize to Kit."

Alice grabbed his arm, "best let it wait a bit Ben, give Buck a good head start."

Ben nods as they head to the kitchen.

Kit was in her room when her mother knocked on her door. She opens the door and slowly comes in. "I thought you could use something to eat since you have been without food for a day." She gently places the tray on her lap and sits down on the nearby chair. "Well I hope this will do, supper will be ready in an hour."

Kit just looks at the dish in her lap, then back to her mother, "I'm really not very hungry Mama. Mama, is Buck downstairs?"

Alice looked down at the floor, she didn't want to tell her daughter he had gone. "No he's in the barn, I believe he told your father he was heading out at dawn."

"Oh Mama, you have to tell Papa not to let him go! They will kill him if they get him!"

"Kill him, for what?"

Kit gets up and starts pacing the room, "when they captured us, they had us tied up and Buck got himself free and when he was trying to free me, a brave came in and they fought. Buck killed him and he got me out and to safety. Oh Mama, you have to make sure he doesn't go back there. They will kill him."

Alice takes Kit in her arms, "there, there Kit, don't worry, nothing will come of Mr. Cross."

Chapter 7

Buck had only been gone a short while when he came across Amos Hunter, Sam Butler and some of their men. He tried to be cordial to them, but it seems they were out for revenge, especially anyone who sided with the Indians. "Good afternoon gentlemen, is there anything I can do for you?"

Amos was the first to speak, "well young fella, seems we meet up again. Mind telling me what you're doing up here?"

Buck smiled, "well I was on my way from the north ridge when I spotted the smoke. I came over to see what it was."

Sam looked at him. "the north ridge, why would you be in the north ridge?"

"Well I was told to go there by Mr. Taylor, and I was always told to do what one's boss says."

A ranch hand behind Buck joins in, "Always doing what your boss says, could it be you was heading there to meet up with your Paiute friends?"

"Paiute friends, what are you talking about?"

Sam answered the question, "that smoke you saw was another farm being burned and another family murdered. Now you wouldn't know about that right?"

The ranch hand slings a rope over Buck's head and tightens it around his waist. "Let's say we give this Indian lover a taste of what he deserves. I say let's string him from the tallest tree."

Amos stops the mob, "I will not stand for any hanging. I don't agree with his ideas on the Indians, but it's no call for us to take the law in our own hands."

Sam looks at Amos, "you mean to tell me, we just let him go?"

The men look at Amos. True he didn't want a hanging over their heads, but he knew they were not going to agree with letting him go. "Alright, rough him up at bit, mind you, not too bad."

With that the ranch hand pulls Buck off the horse and four hands jump on him and start punching him. With his hands under the rope around his waist Buck can't block any of the punches to defend himself. His face soon was covered with blood and cuts to his left, lower lip and his jaw. His shirt was in shreds and from the pain, he assumed a rib or two was broken.

Suddenly there was a shot in the air. When everyone turned, there was Ben on his horse and his rifle aiming at them. Slowly he looked at them, "now nice and easy, you put that young fella on his horse."

Sam looked at him, "Ben the boys were just… They meant no harm."

Ben fired a shot to the ground. "I said put Mr. Cross gently back on his horse."

Two hands put him on the horse.

"Now secure him to the saddle. We don't want him falling now do we? Now one of you young fellas bring the reins over to me."

Amos looks at Ben, "Ben we didn't hurt him too bad, I didn't let them hang him."

Ben looks at the man in disgust, "no you made them beat him. I'm ashamed to say you are my friends. Let me tell you something. This man is a United States Federal Marshall sent here from Washington to find out what is going on out her. Your actions today can not only have you all arrested, but put in prison. I knew you would go too far and now you've done it. Now I'm going to take Mr. Cross home and not only get the doctor and sheriff. I'm having the major at Fort Kearny notified."

Slowly Ben starts his way back down the trail to the farm. With Buck riding beside him, the young man was tied to the saddle with his hands tied to the saddle horn and he was sitting in a slumped position. By the looks of Buck, Ben knew he had to get him home as soon as possible, only in his condition galloping the countryside could kill him. He knew once Buck was at the farm he would make sure the sheriff as was as the major at the fort knew what happened. He still couldn't believe either Amos or Sam, could do such a thing. Why he's known those men for years, they all came to this territory years ago. They've always been fine upstanding citizens.

The sun was beginning to fade as Ben reached the farm, he didn't expect it, but there was Alice standing on the porch. She sees Ben slowly making his way to the house, then she notices Buck slouched in the saddle and calls out to the boys. "Jacob, Eli come out here now!"

Jacob was the first to get out the door, "what is it Mama?"

"Go help your father. Buck's in trouble."

Jacob jumps down the steps and rushes to his dad. "What happened Pa, Indians?"

Slowly Ben gets off his horse, "I'll tell you in a while, first let's get Buck off his horse. Easy now, untie his hands and let's see if we can ease him down on this side."

Jacob gently unties Buck's hands and slowly takes his foot out of the stirrup as Ben takes the boy in his arms. Quickly Jacob rushes over and removes the other foot from the stirrup. Together they make their way to the porch and up the steps.

Alice looks at Eli, "quick, open the door in the store room."

He runs and Ben reaches the top of the porch, "merciful Lord, what happened Ben?"

"I'll tell you later, open the door Alice, this boy needs attention right away!"

Alice opens the door and follows them in. She took one look at Buck's face and gasps. She held her mouth so she wouldn't cry out. She looks at Eli, "Eli get on your horse and get to town get Doc Elliott out here as fast as you can."

The boy nodded and was out the door.

Alice looks at Jacob, "Jacob get some bandages and hot water from the kitchen and fetch me my sewing basket."

He runs out of the room and Ben begins to remove Buck's shirt or what's left of it. It's then that Kit walks into the room. Hearing the noise comes to the doorway, looking in, she sees Buck unconscious and bloody, "oh my Lord, Mama. I told you this would happen. Why would the Paiutes do this to him?"

Ben looks at her, "wasn't the Indians, it was Amos and Sam's ranch hands."

Both women look at him and it was Alice who spoke first, "why?"

"Well, near a I can figure they wanted to string him up for his views on the recent raids and well Amos wanted no part of hanging, so he agreed for the boys to rough him up a bit."

"Rough him up? They darn near killed him. Look at that left eye right over the top, that's gonna need a stich, maybe three, that jaw is in sorry shape, I guarantee you, he's got a few teeth missing and a rib or two broken. But this here on his back, someone took his boot spur and kicked him in the spine. I don't know how much damage that did."

Suddenly Buck begins to stir, "quickly Kit get me the laudanum in the cupboard."

She runs out of the room, "She's not gonna be able to watch this Alice."

Alice looks at her husband, "she will Ben. She's a strong girl."

Kit returned with the laudanum and as Alice administered it to him, Ben removed the rest of his clothes. He started to stir, "Kit, sit there beside him, take his hand, make him know you are there. He has to remain still." Kit sat down beside him and held his hand while Alice tended to his wounds.

It was early in the morning when Eli returned with Dr. Elliott. Jacob led him down the hall and to the back room. He looked at Ben and Alice. "Sorry I was late. Mrs. Carmody's baby wasn't quite sure she wanted to join her six brothers and sisters." He took his coat off and moved a bit closer to the patient. "Well what happened to him?"

Kit stood up, "seems Mr. Hunter and Mr. Butler's ranch hands decided to teach him a lesson."

Doc Elliott gently turned Buck on his side, then looked at Ben, "help me get him on his stomach." The doctor looked at Kit, "Kit I'm afraid you're gonna have to leave for a bit. Alice why don't you both have a rest and Ben and I will handle this."

Alice nodded and took Kit out of the room with her. With the women out of the room the doctor looked at Ben, "I didn't want to alarm the women Ben, but this boy is in bad shape. I can't be sure without opening him if he has damage to his spine. Near as I can figure is, he was kicked in the spine and the spur of the boot dug in and tore either a muscle or tendon of his." He looked up at Ben," now Ben, do you want to tell me what this all about?"

Ben held the lamp closer so the doc could clean the wound. He saw there was a good six – seven-inch gash at his spine that was pretty deep and that's what the doc was worried about. The doc kept talking while tending the wound, "So you want to tell me the story on this one?"

Ben sets the lamp down and looks at the doc, "well Doc, there's not much to tell. You know the Paiute have been raiding the farms along the border and yesterday, me and Butch saw this smoke on the south ridge. He decided to take a look into it. He planned to go to the Paiute village and speak to their chief in hoping he could bring some kind of peace before it was too late."

Doc Elliott looked at him, "is this the story you're going with?"

"You know a different one Doc?"

The doc looks at him, "well yes I do. Let's start with this young man here. He's not a cowhand. He's a Federal Marshall assigned here to not only investigate not only the raids by the Paiute, but also who is supplying the Indians with the guns."

Ben looks at him, "you seem to know quite a bit about this boy."

The doc smiles, "well he is the son of a Kiowa princess and a fur trapper. He was educated in the east by a preacher and his wife. After graduation, he practiced law for a while, then was made a marshal due to his ties with the Kiowa's and his being the grandson of Wise Eagle."

Ben looks at him. "you seem to know a lot about the boy."

"I should, the preacher who educated him was my brother James."

There was a slight tap on the door and Alice sticks her head in, "how is he Doc?"

"Well Alice, I tell you he has a good chance, but I must say he's gonna need a devoted nurse to help him gain his strength. Now I was thinking maybe someone from town. But then, I'd have to move him and..."

Kit rushes into the room, "I'll do it Doc! I can take care of him. I promise."

Alice looks at her, "it's a big job Kit."

"Oh please Mama, I can do it. I promise, I'll take good care of him."

Alice looks at Ben, how could she say no to that face? Alice looks back a Kit, "well as long as you remember not to forget your other chores."

"I won't. I promise. Thank you, Mama."

Doc Elliott looks at her, "now Kit, you have to make sure he gets up three times a day. There's a chance he will not be able to stand up at first. Let him use the crutches. You have to push him to gain strength back in his legs. Now I know what you're thinking, maybe I should take him unto town and have someone stay with him. But I don't want to move him."

Just then Kit comes rushing into the room, "I can do it, I'll take care of him I promise." Alice looks at her, "It's a big job Kit."

Kit looks at him, "Doc, are you saying he can't walk?"

"I'm not saying anything of the sort and I am betting with a pretty gal like you around, he'll be jumping up out of that bed in no time." He looks at Alice, "give him nothing but broth for the next few days, I'll be back on Sunday to check in on him. Oh yes, if he gets restless, give him laudanum to sleep."

Ben looks over to the doc, "how about a cup of coffee Doc?"

"Ya know that sounds fine about now." The three of them leave the room, leaving Kit in there with Buck. She looks at him lying on the bed, his face swollen and bruised. How could they do this to him? He did nothing to them. She moves closer, he hardly looks like he's breathing, but she then noticed his chest slowly raising. She sits down beside him in the nearby chair and gently takes his hand in hers and gently squeezes it. "Don't worry Buck, I'm here and no one will hurt you."

Chapter 8

Just about sunrise, Buck began to stir. He slowly opened his eyes and looks up at the ceiling, then turns his head to see Kit sleeping beside him in the chair still holding on to his hand. He had to admit she did look pretty sitting there. He was afraid to move, fearing he would wake her up, but he needed to move his hand. Slowly he moved it from her grasp and she awakened, "Oh Buck, you're awake. Is something wrong? Are you in pain?"

He smiled at her, "no, no, I'm fine, no, just needed to move my hand. Have you been here all night?"

She smiled and nodded, "well most of it. Can I get you anything?"

"No just sit there. I just enjoy looking at you."

She began to blush. "I'm so glad you are up, I really should go tell the others." She turns to get up when he stops her.

"No not just yet. I'd rather be with you right now no one else."

She sits back down, "alright Buck, if that's what you want." She looks into his eyes, there was such a gentleness there, past those grey eyes, there was a gentle soul and a spirit only a few were allowed to see. The spirit she had fallen in love with.

He slowly tries to move and realizes his legs aren't moving. He looks at her, "Kit, Kit, I can't move my legs! What's wrong?"

"Calm down Buck, Doc says it's only temporary. You had a bad cut on your back and you have to allow that to heal."

He grabs her arm, "how long? How long am I to be like this?"

"I don't know Buck."

Ben, Alice and the doc rush in when they hear Buck yelling. It was Ben who yelled at Kit, "what have you done to the boy?"

Kit looked at her father almost in tears. "I did nothing Papa. He wanted to know how long he would be like this.? I told him I didn't know."

Buck looks at them all, "why didn't any of you tell me about this? Why did you leave a young girl who has no answers in charge of my care? I'm surprised at you Doctor. And you, Mr. Taylor, meaning no disrespect, but you really shouldn't yell at Miss Kit. She didn't know any better."

Kit looks at him, "I didn't know any better! Why you ungrateful piece of donkey dust. I wouldn't take care of you now if you begged me to." She got up and left the room.

Alice was the first to bring back some type of normalcy to the room, "Buck, you've had a very deep cut to your back, the doctor said it will take time to mend, but you also have to understand it cannot be done in a day or two."

He looks at Alice, "I can't stay here until I heal."

"You most certainly can and will. Now that's settled."

He looks at her, "what about Kit, she's really mad?"

Alice smiles at him, "leave her to me." She walks over to the door and calls out to Kit. "Kit, can you come in here?"

Obeying her mother's request, Kit walks in the room. "Kit dear, Mr. Cross would like to apologize for his outburst before."

She looks at Buck.

He looks at Kit, he had to admit she was a pretty one and he wouldn't mind having her as his nurse. "Miss Taylor, I want to apologize for my outburst earlier and I would take it kindly if you would again accept the task of being my nurse until I am healed."

He and everyone else's eyes are on her. "Mr. Cross, I accept your apology and will agree to be your nurse."

Alice smiles, "now if it's alright with the rest of you, let's let the nurse take care of her patient."

Ben looks at her, "but..."

Alice looks at him, "Mr. Taylor, I do believe that we were about to have coffee before all this started, shall we go back to the kitchen?"

With the three of the gone, Buck looks at Kit. "I'm glad you changed your mind."

She smiles at him, "well I kind of feel responsible for all this."

"Responsible? How?"

"Well ever since I met you, you've been captured by Indians, roughed up by ranch hands, I hate to think of what next."

He takes her hand in his, "oh I think it's something to look forward to. Maybe something we will enjoy. It's something to think about."

She had to agree when he put it that way, it was an interesting thought. She looks at him, "well Mr. Cross, I think the first thing we need to do is get you a bit more comfortable."

He smiles at her as she proceeds to fluff up his pillows. "Are you always going to be so formal?"

She turns and straightens the covers, "I don't know what you mean."

He gently grabs her hand and slowly pulls her down to him until their faces are inches apart, "I mean my lovely Kit, you will never be Miss Taylor in my eyes."

She moved closer and smiled at him, "and what am I in your eyes?"

He gently places a kiss on her lips, then releases her, "you're always my Kit."

She looks at him and somehow the look in his eyes tells her he means it.

Later that afternoon, Kit starts helping Buck with his exercise. "Alright Buck, you've been in that bed long enough, let's get you to stand up."

"Stand up?" He looked at her. "Stand up?"

"I believe that's what I said."

"But Kit, I'm…"

She puts her arms under his shoulders and lifts him up. Tucking the crutches under his shoulders, she waits until he is balanced before moving back. "See, you're standing!"

He looks at her, "now what?"

"Nothing, just stand, we need to get the blood circulating and since that can only happen if you are standing that's what we are doing."

He tries to move closer to her and begins to lose his balance. "Kit!"

She grabs him and puts her arms around him breaking his fall. "It's alright, I got you."

He looks at her, "here I am in the arms of a beautiful women and I have nothing to say."

Kit looks at him, "okay Buck, let's get back into bed, slowly."

He smiles, "back into bed?"

"Back." She pushes him gently and she falls with him, landing on top of him, he gently places a kiss on her lips. "You know Miss, you are a hard woman to say, know."

"Then I suggest you don't Mr. Cross."

Chapter 9

The following morning, Ben and Jacob head into town to see the sheriff and Matt Hollister. As they rode, they are met by Amos Hunter. "Morning Ben, how's the young boy doing?"

"It's still too early to tell. Doc says, it seemed some with spurs from some boots gave him some hard kicks to his back. Sliced open a huge cut and he won't know for sure until it heals if he can walk again."

Amos just shook his head," that's too bad, but I did stop them from stringing him up."

Ben looked at him, "well when his grandpa finds out, make sure someone tells him that."

"His grandpa?"

Ben smiles, "oh, did I forget to mention Buck is the grandson of Chief Yellow Moon of the Kiowa nation?"

"His grandpa is…"

"Yep, and as I heard it, he's the only grandson of the ole chief."

Suddenly Amos feels he needs to get home, more than that, he has to tell this information to Sam and Bill, "well Ben, I hope the boy recovers, I best get moving on. You take care of yourself." With that Amos rides off back to his ranch.

Jacob looks at his pa, "Pa, you suppose Mr. Hunter is gonna tell the others?"

Ben smiles at his son. "I'm betting on it Jake,"

Soon after Ben and Jacob arrive at the sheriff's office. They walk in and Pat Cullen is sitting at his desk. "Afternoon Ben, Jacob, what can I do you for?"

Ben stands in front of his desk, "well for one thing, I would like to press charges against Amos Hunter, Sam Butler and their men for the brutal attack on Mr. Buck Cross."

"Well Ben, what do you mean by brutal attack?"

"It seems the ranch hands carried their fun too far when they beat Mr. Cross, leaving him quite possibly unable to walk ever again. How will that look to the officials in Washington."

"Washington?"

"Pat, you do understand that Cross is a federal marshal, don't you? You do understand that they must be charged and tried for their actions."

Pat looks at him, "you're telling me this Buck Cross is a marshal and …"

He's not just a federal marshal, he's also the grandson of Yellow Moon, chief of the Kiowa nation. He's the only grandson of the ole boy."

"Do you think we're looking at a war from the Kiowa?"

"There's a chance, but I'd be more worried at who's supplying rifles to the Indians."

"Well you're just full of information today ain't you? Which one do you want me to check first?"

"I would appreciate it if you would handle the complaint on the ranch hands first. If the judge can make them pay for what they have done to him, maybe the boy won't find a way to get revenge on his own."

Pat looks at him, "you can't mean…."

"Pat this is the grandson of a chief beaten by white men what do you think?" Ben heads for the door.

"You leaving Ben?"

"I feel I should tell the major what happened. He at least may be able to help us if the boy takes a turn for the worst." Ben has his hand on the door knob.

Pat gets up, "now Ben, don't go doing anything rash and for God sakes, don't try to take this on by yourself."

"You just do your job Pat and don 't worry about me." He leaves the office and heads for the fort.

On the south ridge, Bill Franks gathers with a small group of his men. They were only six in total and three covered wagons. Each wagon had a driver and another to ride shotgun. At the beginning of the pass, Bill stops the wagons and looks all around. Within minutes, the pass is filled with Paiutes and they follow the men into the pass.

Once in the pass, an Indian brave rides up to Franks and speaks to him. "You have the guns?"

Franks smiles, "just like I promised you, they're in the wagon." He motions for his men to open the crates, "pass them out boys." He grabs one and hands it to Wise Buffalo. "With these Wise Buffalo, your people could take many cows and drive the whites away from this land."

The brave looks at him, "you have kept your promise Franks, you have done good for my people with these, my people will be able to wipe out the whites forever."

Franks is pleased that Wise Buffalo is happy. He looks at the chief, "the next farm you are to raid is the Morgan farm. It's the little one in the bottom of the valley. Take the cattle into the hills for your people. Make sure no one is left alive."

Wise Buffalo still admiring the rifle in his hand when Franks looks at him, "remember, no one left alive."

"I have heard your words Franks, no one will be left alive."

Back at the fort, Ben again is explaining to the major what happened to Buck. The major had already heard a story though not the same from Bill Franks. Though the major felt the Franks story didn't seem to have some convincing truth to it. There were too many demands on Franks part and the fact the rancher's hand been using the Indian lands to graze their cattle all this time. Using the land and wondering why the Indians were raiding their ranches and taking off with the rest of their cattle.

Ben looks at the major, "I'm afraid the raids will continue Major, until Mr. Cross is able to get back on his feet again."

"Back on his feet?"

Ben looked at him, "yes, I came to town today to have charges placed on the ranch hands of the Hunter, Butler and Franks ranches as well as the three men for the brutal beating of United States Federal Marshal Buck Cross."

The major raises from his chair, "they did what? Why wasn't I told about this?"

Ben looks at him, "I have no idea why, but I'm telling you now!"

The major walks to the door of his office and calls to his orderly. "Sergeant Crawford, get me Captain Sanders immediately." He walks back to his desk, sits down and looks at Ben. "You are telling me these men attacked and beat up a federal marshal and no one stopped it? Does anyone realize the punishment for a crime of this nature? Thy are looking at a year in prison."

While the major was drawing up the papers on the men involved to give to the sergeant to serve on them, the Paiute's were attacking the Morgan farm. They made sure the Morgan's were killed along with their two ranch hands.

Chapter 10

News of the attack on the Morgan families and many of the settlers were getting uneasy. It was now the settlers were looking to the Army for protection and more than that, to drive the Paiutes out of the territory. It was Bill Franks who spoke out on how the Army was here to protect them and they should run the Indians out of that land. He was the first to spread the news of the raid on the Morgan farm, and inciting the mob to march on the Sheriff and demand action. It was Franks standing at the door of the sheriff's office shouting for protection when Pat walks out.

"Well Franks, you have my attention, now what do you want me to do?"

Bill steps up to him, "we want you to do your job and to get rid of these heathen Indians and make this territory safe again. Take back that land, they don't deserve it."

Pat looks at the crowd, "am I to assume all of you agree with Bill Franks here."

There was talking in the crowd that the land should be taken from the Indians. A voice in the crowd yelled out, "give us the land."

Pat looks out in the crowd knowing who shouted that comment, "look you all don't seem to understand, this all was their land to start with, we are the ones who took it from them."

Franks decided to get them agitated, "they don't want it and we should have it!"

Pat looks at Franks, then back to the crowd, "now I'm only gonna say this one time, Washington has sent a marshal out here to find out what's going on. Trouble is, he was attacked and beaten and is in pretty bad shape right now."

Franks yells into the crowd, "another lie. All they do is tell us lies."

Pat spoke up," well this is no lie Mr. Franks, I have warrants for the arrests of the hands of the Hunter and Butler ranches for what they did to Buck Cross."

Bill looks at him, "you have no proof of that."

"Ben Taylor came in himself this morning to make the complaint himself and Doc. Elliott signed the paper. He treated the boy. Now if y'all don't want to join the others, I suggest y'all go back to your homes and leave this up to the law."

Ben and Jacob made their way to Matt Hollister's place about 10 miles from town, since it was on their way home they decided to stop and pay Matt a visit. As they rode up to the house, Ben noticed Matt standing on the porch with his rifle in his hand. As they drew closer Matt raised his gun, "who goes there?"

Ben and Jacob stop and raised their hands, "I's me, Ben Taylor and Jacob, Matt."

Matt lowers his rifle, "sorry Ben, can't be too careful these days."

Ben and Jacob get off their horses, "Been having trouble Matt?"

"I tell you Ben, I have no idea what's gotten into folk. Two weeks ago, Bill Franks comes out here and tells me he'd be willing to have his cattle graze with mine since we're having all the trouble with the Paiutes. I told him my cattle were fine where they were, but thanked him for the offer. Three days later, ten of my best steers were found with arrows in them. Now you know as well as me, Indians wouldn't kill them steers and leave em there. Ben, them cows were killed by white men."

"Well I just come from the fort and the sheriff's office, Amos and Sam's boys had a good time teaching Buck Cross a lesson. They would have killed him if I hadn't stopped it."

Matt looked at him, "they rough the boy pretty bad?"

Ben nods his head, "the jury is still out if he'll be able to walk."

Matt shakes his head, "that's a shame, he seems like a good enough boy."

"Well he had to be, he's a marshal."

"Still have his horse here, leg is pretty much healed. Pretty young thing."

Ben looks at him, "someone is trying to get the Paiute land in the process, trying to drive them out of the territory. They may get more than they bargained for. Buck is the grandson of Kiowa Chief Yellow Moon."

Matt looked at him, "Yellow Moon! No wonder Washington sent him here. There's been talk the Kiowa and the Paiutes may join up. I hope he recovers, no matter who his grandpa is. Do you know he paid me in advance to take care of his horse? I told him I'd lend him one till his got better, but he said he was fine with walking'."

Ben nodded, "that's the same day he met Kit on the trail and she took him home that night."

It was late afternoon when Kit came back into Buck's room with his lunch. The smile on his face fades as seem his lunch is a bowl of broth.

Kit looks at him, "is something Mr. Cross?"

"Yes Miss Tylor, how does one expect to regain my strength if I'm only fed broth?"

"I'm sorry Mr. Cross, Doctor's orders, only broth until he comes on Sunday."

He looks at her, "Sunday! I'll be dead by then!"

She gives him a smile, "oh I doubt that very much." She turns to leave when she hears him pick up the spoon. She smiles and heads out the door.

Buck looks at her leave and shakes his head, she was something else he had to admit.

Chapter 11

Back at Amos Hunter's ranch, Amos tells both Sam and Bill what Ben had told him earlier that afternoon. Bill was the first to comment, "I knew he was a marshal. The major at the fort told me."

Amos looks at him, "well you better know the second half, seems the boy is grandson to Chief Yellow Moon of the Kiowa nation. Now I'm thinking if the chief knows what we've done to his grandson he ain't gonna be too happy. I'm pretty sure he's gonna wanna know who these people are."

Bill was quick to answer, "well that's why the Army's here. If we have an Indian problem, we get them to run those savages out of the land and then there will be more for all of us."

Amos looks at him, "what about the families if the Indians attack? We've buried the Henderson's and the Morgan's, who will be next?"

Sam now joins in, "they wouldn't attack if the Army was here."

Bill looks at him, "that's just it Sam, the Army won't come unless they get a report from that Cross fella, and he's in no shape to move anywhere, thanks to all of us."

Amos adds, "that's not the only problem."

"What else?"

"Ben has pressed charges on all of us for what happened to the boy. He's got Pat serving us the papers this afternoon."

Bills smiles, "well he can't blame this one on me. I was at the fort when it all took place."

Sam looked at him, "no your hands weren't here, but your hands were, the cowboy who suggested the beating was your top hand Josh."

Just then the sound of a horse riding up to the farm is heard and Amos looks out the window to see it's Pat Cullen. He gets off his horse and heads up the stairs and to the door.

"It's Pat."

Bill heads toward the window to make his getaway. "I'm not getting caught for something I wasn't part of. You two were there, not me." He opens the window and climbs out and makes his way around the front of the house just as Pat was knocking in the door.

As Amos answers Pat's knock, Bill quietly walks his horse, so he could leave without being noticed.

"Well howdy Pat, come on in."

"I appreciate it Ben, is Bill and Sam in there with ya?"

"Why yes, Sam is here, but I ain't seen Bill at all today. What's this all about?"

They walk into the parlor where Sam gets up to greet Pat. "Good to see ya Pat."

"You may not say that after I hand you both these papers." He reached in his pocket and pulled three pieces of paper. Looking at them, he places one back in his pocket and looks at them as he hands each one.

"What's this?"

Pat looks at Sam, "Well Sam, it seems these are charges brought out on you, Amos, Bill and your hands for the beating of Ben Cross, U.S. Federal Marshall of this territory."

Sam looks at him, "now Pat, how come we..."

Pat held up his hand for Sam to stop. "Sam I'm only delivering these. Ben Taylor made the charges and you can hash it out with Judge Walsh in two weeks when he gets here."

"You mean we're to be in jail for two weeks?"

"Just don't try to leave the territory Sam, that's all." As he's about to leave he looks at both of them," you wouldn't know if Bill is at his place would ya?"

They both shake their heads.

He just shakes his head, "I'll just have to see for myself. Don't forget you and your hands in town in two weeks. Don't let me cone out and get you." With that he heads out of the room and out the door.

Thirty miles east of the Amos farm is the small farm of Chris and Ada Killum. Chris was a simple man, both he and the Mrs. never went into town much, usually once a month for supplies. They had no children, but they had each other. Never feeling he needed more than what the good Lord wanted him to have, he was thankful he had his Ada and nothing else mattered.

Ada was in the house placing the dishes on the table for supper when the Indians attacked. They killed her instantly and proceeded to set fire to the house. When Chris heard the screams, he raced out of the barn only to be faced with the braves who shot him with arrows. They then went into the barn and took the stock and headed once again across to their territory.

Back at the Taylor farm, Eli came rushing in to tell his pa he saw smoke in the far distance.

Ben raced out with both boys behind him. It was true, there was smoke in the far south where the Killum farm was. He looked at Eli, "Son fetch my gun, Jacob, saddle the horses."

Eli ran into the house as Alice ran out from the kitchen. She sees Eli get his father's gun and rush back out of the house. She follows him and sees him hand Ben his gun, "here ya go Pa."

Alice looks at Ben, "Ben where are you going?"

"Alice it looks as though they got the Killum farm. I'll go with Jacob to see if they need some help."

Eli comes running up with his horse. "Can I go too Pa?"

Ben looks at the boy, "no son, I would like you to stay here with your ma and Kit."

"But Pa!"

"I need a man I can trust to take care of the women folk and right now you're that man Eli. So will you do it son?"

"Yes, sir."

"That's my boy." He smiles at Alice, "we'll be back as soon as we check this out."

Jacob hands him the horses and reins and as Ben mounts his horse they head off.

Alice puts her hand on Eli's shoulder, "one day Eli, you'll be riding out with them." Slowly they walk back into the house, not realizing they are being watched by two Paiute braves and Bill Franks. He looks at the two Indians, "inside the house is the grandson of Yellow Moon, if we should capture him and take him back to his grandfather, Yellow Moon would be very grateful. He looks at the braves, "you both go back to Spotted Calf, tell him I will bring the grandson of Yellow Moon with me back to the camp before the end if this day." He quickly and quietly moves toward the house and around the back to find an opened window to sneak in. It would be so easy to get Cross, after all, with two women and a young boy to protect him, he could walk out the front door with no resistance.

From the window of his room, Buck sees the two Indians on the ridge and another figure. As the other figure turns, Buck sees it is Bill Franks. For a man who professed so many times they were savages, he was sure nice to them up there on the ridge. Could he be the supplier for the rifles? But for what purpose? His attention was distracted as Kit walked into the room.

"Kit come over here. I want you to look up that ridge."

"Buck why would I…" She stands behind him, "Buck isn't that Mr. Franks? Why is he with those Indians? Buck?"

"Kit I want you to tell Eli he has to go find your pa and Jacob now! Tell him we need them back here!"

"But Buck, what's wrong? Why does Eli…"

He takes her hands in his, "Kit I need you to remain calm, I want you to find Eli and tell him what I told you." He saw the look of fright on her face.

"Buck, you don't think…"

"If I'm right they only want me, no one else."

"Buck they can't take you, why you can't even walk."

"No, but I still can shoot. Now there's one more thing I need you to do, I want you to take your mother and both of you go into the root cellar and don't come out until you hear me or your pa's voice."

"Root cellar, no Buck you…"

He places his hands on her shoulders, "promise me Kit."

"Buck, I'm not leaving you here alone."

"You'll do what I say."

"I will not leave you."

He pulls her to him and takes her in his arms, "you will do as I say Kathrine. Can't you understand, I'm trying to protect you?"

She tries to pull free from his embrace, "let me go Buck."

He smiles at her, "you really are gonna be impossible to live with, aren't you? Maybe I should think twice about asking for your hand in marriage."

Still trying to get free, Kit stops when she hears what he had just said. She looks up at him, "asking for my hand?"

He lifts his hand close to her mouth, "I thought you'd get it sooner or later." He gently places a kiss on her lips.

"Buck you ain't funning' me, are you?"

"I may joke about a lot of things, but never something but never something as important as this."

"But Buck, we hardly know each other."

"And can't think of a better way to get to know each other."

"Buck Cross you are..."

He kisses her. "Well it seems I found a way to keep you quite. I must say a very pleasurable way too."

She pulls away from him and stands up, "you are not fair Mr. Cross."

"I'm glad you like the name, it does have a nice sound to it, Katherine Cross."

"That's something that will never happen Mr. Cross."

"Now now, never say never sweet Kit. Now go tell Eli what I said and then both you and your mom go to the root cellar."

She leaver the room and Buck goes back to looking out the window. By this time Franks and the two Indians are gone. Talking to no one in particular, "okay, where did you three disappear to now?"

From behind him he hears Frank's voice, "right behind you Cross." Standing there is Franks with his gun aimed right at Buck.

Buck looks at his gun on the night table, too far for him to reach. "Well, see you have me at a disadvantage Mr. Franks. May I ask where are your two friends?"

"I sent them back to Spotted Calf."

"And the women?"

"Oh well, let's just say I saw Kit taking her mom to the root cellar. Now if you don't mind, I do feel we must get on our way."

"May I ask where?"

Franks smiles, "why to see your grandfather of course. I'm sure he would like to see his grandson."

Buck looked at him, "you know you're crazy, don't you? My grandfather is a good three days ride from here and last I heard the Kiowa were not on friendly terms with the whites."

"Oh but he would be friendly, after all I'm taking you to him."

Buck looked at him, "you don't understand my grandfather."

"Maybe not, but I know his grandson and I know he wouldn't do anything to hurt the Taylor family especially the one called Kit." Franks saw the look on Buck's face, "I see I touched a nerve, then we can agree on this. Now get up and let's get moving."

Buck looks at him, "you're behind all these raids, aren't you? What type of sick demented person are you? Watching your friends and neighbors being killed for no reason at all."

Bill looks at him, "you don't get it do you boy. You see we all came out here to this territory after the war since we lost everything. The government gave us this fine offer of free land and we took it. Then we find out they gave the same land to the Indians. The Indians, can you believe that, why those savages don't even use it.

That's when I figured why not let our stock graze on it. After all the Indians don't use it."

Buck looks at him, "Just what does all this have to do with my grandfather?"

"Simple, your grandpa and all the Indians feel a war is the only way to get rid of the whites. I am interested in the land, so I supply them with the guns to fight this war, in this way everyone gets what they want.

Buck looks at him, "and it doesn't matter to you how many innocent lives, whites and Indians, that are lost?"

"Oh come on now boy, there are no innocent Indians, hell look what they did to Custer and his men."

"Look what Custer did to those at Washita!"

Franks looks at him. "And I don't think they should have the land. Now let's just get up from that chair and make our way to the door."

Buck looks at him, "well I'm sorry to disappoint you, but there is one small problem. I can't walk. Your hands did work on my back real well. Seems one of them had spurs and well, when he kicked his spurs cut into my flesh and did quite a bit of damage."

"You'll get up or I'll drag you out of this room. Do you hear me?" He grabs Buck's hand and pulls him out of the chair causing him to fall on the floor when he slid out of the chair. Slowly he begins to drag Buck to the door.

From the hall Kit comes running in with a rifle in her hand and she aims it at Franks. "Mr. Franks, I would suggest you take your hand from Mr. Cross' arm or I may be forced to shoot it off. And if ya'll have any doubts whether I can do it or not, it wouldn't be a good idea to question it. I never miss what I aim at." Franks looks at her, "you're bluffing."

Suddenly she pulls the trigger and the fringe on the sleeve of his jacket goes flying through the air. She aims at his hand and looks at him, "next time, I will aim straight at your hand and see it fly like the fringe did."

Franks let's go of Buck's hand and Buck slowly crawls to the chair. Kit looks at Buck, "take your time Buck, Mr. Franks ain't going nowhere."

Franks looks at her, "you're making a big mistake young lady, and you'll be sorry."

Kit smiles at him, "looks like you've made the mistake Mr. Franks. As for me, well, I heard the sounds of someone in the house and when I came to Buck's room, I saw you had your gun aimed at him. I shot to stop you from
shooting Buck."

Franks looked at her, "kill Cross? I don't even have my gun in my hand."

"That can be fixed once I shoot you. The others would find the gun in your hand."

Suddenly the sounds of horses coming at a fast pace approach. Ben and the boys are back. Ben jumps off his horse followed by Jacob and Eli and rushes into the house. Ben shouts out, "Alice, Kit! Where are you?"

Kit yells out from the back room not taking her aim off Franks, "back here Papa."

Ben makes his way to the back room and sees Kit with Buck and Franks. "what the heck is going on here?" Ben looks at Kit, "Kit what are you doing?"

"Well you see Papa, Mr. Franks here, he seems to feel the Paiutes don't deserve the land and he figured to have the Indians and the whites go to war and he would end up with all the land." She looks over to Franks, "am I getting it right so far?"

Franks just bows his head and nods.

Ben looks over at Buck, "you alright son?"

Buck nods and Ben looks back at Franks, "you were willing to start a war just for land? What type of person goes against his own kind? You let your hired hands beat this boy so bad…"

Franks shakes his head, "come on Ben, you know Injins are used to beatings, they do it to each other all the time."

Ben looks at him, "you realize if his grandpa sees what the whites have done, there will be a war."

"That's why I planned to take the boy to his grandpa. He'll want those responsible to pay for what was done to him."

Ben looks at him, "and I suppose since you are the one bringing his grandson to him, you would be grateful for some reward for your effort."

"Well of course."

Suddenly Alice comes rushing in the room and runs to Ben. "Oh Ben, thank God you're here. We were so worried. I was so worried about Kit, she didn't want to stay with me."

Kit looks at her mother, "I'm fine Mama and so is Buck. Mr. Franks here is behind it all."

Alice looks at Franks, "Bill, why? What could you gain by having your friends killed? Why you lost your own Maude coming out here. We all stood by you when she passed."

He looked at her, "you wouldn't understand Alice, no one would."

Slowly Jacob and Eli took Franks from the room and Ben walks out with his wife leaving Kit and Buck alone. Before he leaves, he takes the rifle from Kit's hand and tosses it gently to Buck, I think you should hang in to this son."

Buck smiles at Ben, then looks at Kit, "I think you're right sir."

Chapter 12

Ben and the boys ride into town that afternoon taking Franks to the sheriff's office, saving Pat the trip to come out and get him. After locking him behind bars, Ben proceeds to tell Pat what Franks was planning and how he was responsible for all the raids.

Pat gets up from his chair and pours himself a cup of coffee. "I tell you Ben, I've known you, Franks and the rest of you since we came out to this territory. We all had dreams and hopes, we came out here to forget the war and leave all that behind us. To start a new life. Seems Franks never could. He wanted more and would stop at nothing to get it. He changed after Maude died. It wasn't the Indians who killed her," he looked over at Ben, "she was a frail little bit of a thing. Why even the doctors told him not to take her. Told him to leave her in Ohio until she got stronger. But once again, Franks had to do things his way. He said the mountain air would help her. She never made it to the mountains."

Ben nodded as he remembered he and Amos dug Maude's grave. Somewhere out on the trail a simple cross marker shows where Maude Franks was laid to rest.

Back at the farm, Buck stays close to the window while Alice and Kit are in the kitchen. For some reason he doesn't feel they are out of danger yet. He feels it because of who he is. He feels Spotted calf is going to make an appearance some time and he wants it to be on his terms. He notices movement near the corral and as Kit walks into the room. He looks at Kit and in a low voice says, "Kit, blow out the candle and walk back out of the room."

"But Buck, it's almost…"

"Kit, for once in your life don't argue. Take your mother and go to the upstairs bedroom closest to the far side if the house."

She looks at him." Indians?"

He just nods. "Oh Buck, I just want to…"

He grabs her arm, "you will do as I say."

She looks at him, "but Buck…"

"Kit I need you to listen, it's important." He smiles at her," don't worry, you won't lose me..."

She leaves the room and with Alice they quickly go up the stairs and to the bedroom Buck had told her to go.

Quietly he waited as he heard the sound of rustling leaves as the braves moved closer to the house. Propped in his chair with his rifle resting on the window ledge allowing only a small amount of the barrel showing out the window, he sits and waits. So many thoughts race through his head, *what if they manage to get through. How could he protect Kit and her mother with the way he is? Could he make sure they remained safe upstairs?* Suddenly he heard the window in the far end of the hall begin to open. He held his breath and watched a shadowy figure climb in. Slowly he moved his rifle from the window and as the second figure climbed in he aimed and fired. He aimed again and fired as the other fell at the foot of the stairs.

Upstairs Alice held on to Kit who wanted to head down the stairs. "Kit he said to stay here."

"Mama, you don't understand, he may need help."

"He told you to stay here, you can't help him if he has to worry about you."

"But Mama, what can I do?"

"Ask the good Lord to help him and pray your father and the boys come back soon."

Downstairs, three more shots rang out, flashes of light, then it was silent again. When Buck was sure there were no more braves, he called out to Kit.

She came racing down passed the dead braves and into Buck's arms. "Oh Buck, I was so worried." She held him tighter.

"Now didn't I tell you I would be alright."

She looked up at him, even in the darkness she could see his face, his smile, his eyes.

He bends down and gently kisses her, "I told ya, you ain't gonna lose me."

Slowly Alice made it down the stairs and when her foot touched the lifeless body of the Indian she let out a cry.

Kit jumped, "Mama? Mama, are you alright?"

"Yes, yes, is Buck alright?"

Buck answered, "Yes Mrs. Taylor, I'm fine, thank you."

Once she passed the hall, Alice had no problem getting to the back room where Buck and Kit were. As she reached the room, Kit was lighting the lamp. She looked at Buck, "thank God, you are safe I hate to think of what would have happened if we were alone. Do you know why they came here?"

"I suppose they were looking for Franks. He promised to give me to the man, well, he didn't deliver, they came looking."

"But why?"

"Spotted Calf is an old friend of sorts, we knew each other many years ago. He spent time in my grandfather's village and as Franks pointed out to him, to have the grandson of Yellow Moon would be powerful medicine for any warrior."

Kit looked at him," I'm just glad they didn't get you." She puts her hand in his and he gently kisses it.

"I'm glad too."

The sound of horses riding up drew their attention to the window. Buck looked up as he saw Ben and the boys get off their horses.

Ben yelled out, "Alice! Kit! Where are you?"

"In here Papa!"

Hearing this, Ben raced into the house. He tripped over one of the dead Indians as he rushed to the back room. "Kit!"

He reaches the bedroom and Alice rushes to him. "Oh Ben, I'm so glad you're here."

He puts his arms around her and tries to comfort her, and looks over to Buck who is still holding Kit's hand. He nods to him.

Alice looks up at her husband, "It was just terrible Ben. Buck was wonderful. He told us to go upstairs and he stayed down here and… Oh Ben, he was just wonderful."

Ben looked at Buck, "thank you son."

"You're welcome sir. But I only did what had to be done."

"You protected what is very precious to me."

Buck looks at Kit, "believe me, I know how precious they are."

After that day Ben never questioned Buck's feelings for Kit.

The following morning, Kit walked into the kitchen and sees Alice has already started breakfast. "You're up early Mama."

Alice looks over and sees Kit is pouring herself a cup of coffee. "Well I had a hard time sleeping, so I came down here and started breakfast early. If you'd like to bring something to Buck I think he's up."

"Good idea," she pours another cup of coffee and heads to Buck's room.

As she does, Ben walks in. "Good morning Kit."

He sees the cup of coffee and smiles, "oh is this for me, thank you." He takes the cup and heads for the table.

Kit walks back and again makes a cup of coffee.

Alice looks at Ben, "Ben why did you take Buck's cup of coffee."

Ben looks at her, "Kit gave it to me. If I had known it was…"

"No, no Papa, it's alright. I can get him another."

Suddenly the door to Buck's room opens and slowly Buck makes his way out on crutches.

Kit turns and calls his name, "Buck!"

He holds his hand up for her to stay where she is, "Stay there Kit. If I need help, I'll let you know." Slowly he begins to move one foot, then the other. He begins to lose his balance and Kit rushes to him. She puts his arm around her shoulder and grabs his waist. When he starts to object, she looks at him, "let me help you this time Buck."

"Alright you win," she helps him over to the chair and eases him down.

Alice comes over with a plate of eggs and bacon and places it before him, "now you eat this and your days of broth are over."

He smiles up at her, "if I knew that I would have gotten out of the room last week."

With that everyone was laughing.

Chapter 13

Back in the village of Spotted Calf, the fact that the braves had not come back with the grandson of Yellow Moon displeases the young chief. Also the one named Franks has not returned the rifles he had promised to bring. Something was wrong, yet to take a small party to the home of Franks would be a foolish move. Perhaps Franks had changed his mind. Perhaps he planned to do his trading with Yellow Moon. Many questions raced through his mind yet none of them had answers.

As Kit helps her mother with the wash, the women don't seem to notice they are being watched. Slowly and quietly a small band of braves make their way toward the back yard. As Buck was sitting on the back porch watching the women, he saw the flash of movement from the corner of his eye. He knew they were not alone and he had to get the women inside to safety. "Ahh ladies, I'm beginning to get a bit tired, can I ask you both to help me get back inside?"

Kit looked at him, "does it have to be right now? I mean we're almost finished."

Buck smiles at her, "well, I am very tired and I think it's too warm out here." Without saying another word he moves his eyes toward the left where the braves are.

Kit looks at him and then to her mother, "Mama, I think we should help Buck back inside, he's really been in the sun too long."

Alice looks at him, "he does seem a bit flushed." They both walk over and help him to his feet. As they make their way to the door an arrow cuts through the air and lands on the door frame. Alice screams and Buck pushes both her and Kit inside and closes the door, leaving him outside. He turns and sees Spotted Calf standing there. Holding on to one crutch Buck tries to balance himself.

"It seems my brother Lone Wolf is injured."

"Oh it's not too bad, I am getting stronger each day."

"Is this how the white men treat the grandson of Yellow Moon?"

"Not all of them, just Bill Franks."

"You are saying Franks did this to you?"

"Not himself, his men."

Spotted Calf smiled at him, "it has been too long since we were together at your grandfather's village. Do you remember what our life was back then?"

"That was a long time ago."

"Was it so long ago that Lone Wolf forgot who he is?"

"It seems Spotted Calf forgets I also am half white."

"I have not forgotten, but you seemed to have forgotten your Kiowa side. It's time you once again join your people and lead them against the whites who are driving all of us off our land."

He looked at the brave, as boys they were good friends, but boys grow up and soon make their own paths and destiny. Buck chose to follow the path of his father's people.

Spotted Calf looked at him, "you like this white man's life?"

"It's the one I chose."

"You like the white woman?"

"She is a friend."

"A friend you would take as your woman one day."
"I hadn't thought…"

Spotted Calf looks at him in anger, "you lie, my braves have watched you, how you look at her, how you protect her."

"I protect her because she is my friend."

"If she is your friend, let her come out here to me. Let me be her friend also."

Buck looks at the brave. He knew he was at a disadvantage, but he also knew he had to protect Kit.

"Well Lone Wolf, I am waiting."

Suddenly the door opens and Kit slowly walks out. Buck looks at her in surprise, but Kit just smiles and nods her head. Spotted Calf smiles, his facial gestures show he is pleased at what he sees. "My braves did not tell me how beautiful she is. I would gladly give you four of my best horses for her."

Kit looks at Buck.

Buck looks at him, "she is not for sale."

Again Spotted Calf gives him a bid, "I will give you six ponies for her."

Buck takes her arm and pulls her close to him, "no ponies, she is not for sale."

Spotted Calf looks at her, then back to Buck, "it seems Lone Wolf wants to keep the little white squaw for himself. I will wait and when I kill you Lone Wolf, I will take that little squaw for my own and anything else you have."

Buck could feel Kit's arm tense up and Spotted Calf begins to back away. "Until we meet again Lone Wolf." With that he was gone.

Kit looks at Buck and he holds on to her as he starts to weaken, "let's get inside."

She grabs his waist and helps him in the house.

From now on there would be a guard watching the house at all times. One thing Buck knew for sure was

Spotted Calf would return and would surely keep his threat the next time.

Back at the Paiute village, Spotted Calf had a visitor that was made welcome. A mighty and powerful chief who had come to the village to find out the stories he has heard about his grandson. As others sat outside the teepee, inside Yellow Moon was listening about his grandson and how he has turned against his people and rode with the whites.

Yellow Moon looked at Spotted Calf, "I have heard many stories, stories of how my grandson has forgotten his people, I heard he walks among the whites as one of them. I heard he is no longer proud of his Kiowa blood."

Spotted Calf nods, "it is true great one, he no longer acts like a Kiowa. He has taken a new name to be more like them."

Yellow Moon looks down at the fire, "it saddens me to think of the boy I raised turn against all he stands for. I had hoped he would be proud of what he was and take his place in the tribe when the time came…" His thoughts drifted as he sadly had to believe what he had been told to by Spotted Calf. He looks up at the brave, "I must speak with Lone Wolf."

"I can have a brave go to the place he is and send a message you are requesting him here."

"Let it be done."

Sitting on the porch the following morning, Buck looks up at Kit, "you do know I would never let Spotted Calf take you."

She looked at him and smiled, "and here I thought you were holding out for more horses."

He pulls her to him and sits her on his lap. She was so close to him he could feel the beat of her heart. "Do you always get this excited when you sit on a man's lap?"

She moves closer to him and just inches away from his mouth, "only when it's close to someone I care very much about."

He gently kisses her, then pulls back, "so I'm guessing you care about me." She pulls him closer to her again. "Buck Cross, sometimes you talk too much," and she kisses him.

Ben walks out the door and clears his throat.

Kit looks up and sees he father and blushes. "Ahh, this was... I mean I was…"

A smile came to Ben's face, "I think I can understand Kit. It may come as a shock to you, but I have been known to have done that sort of thing a few times."

Kit's face at this time is beet red as she scrambles off Bucks lap and runs into the house. Both of them found it amusing.

They begin to laugh when Buck sees smoke over by the south ridge. "Ben!" Buck looks at Ben, "it's not a fire Ben it's signal."

"A signal for who?"

Buck looks at him. "it's for me. I have to go to the Paiute village."

"You can't go anywhere… how long do you think you would be able to fake the fact you can't walk?"

Buck looks at him, "Ben, if I don't go, I will never have the chance to stop these raids and save my people from being destroyed."

"Well you're not going alone, I'm going with you."

Buck looks at him, "I can't let you do that Ben, if I don't come back you'll be needed here to take care of Alice and Kit." Buck tries to get up and falls back into the chair.

Ben looks at him, "sure you are gonna save all the problems. You can't even get out of the chair." As Ben's voice gets louder, Kit and Alice come out the door.

Alice looks at them, "what are you two carrying on about now?"

Ben looks at his wife, "Buck thinks he's going alone to the Paiute village."

Kit looks at him, "he most certainly is not."

Ben smiles. "see!"

Kit looks at him, "I'm going with him."

The smile on Ben's face changes, "you are not going up there."

Kit looks at both men, "look let's face it, you can see Buck is in no shape to walk and you know you will not get near the village Dad, so I am the perfect choice. Besides Spotted Calf wouldn't let anything happen to me."

Buck looks at her and shook his head. "I don't like the idea and I don't want you near that village,"

Chapter 14

As they were discussing the matter, a single Paiute brave came to the farm carrying a white flag. He wanted to speak to Buck with a message from his grandfather. He proceeded to tell Buck his grandfather wants to speak with him. A common ground was established which was near the stream that separates the Indian land and the south border of the Taylor farm. The meeting was set for the following day when the sun was in the middle of the sky. Buck was allowed to take one with him and Yellow Moon would take one. The brave went back with the time and conditions to agree on.

Ben looked at Buck, "I don't like it Buck, I can't trust these…"

Buck looked at him, "savages Ben? Is that what you were going to say?"

Ben put his head down, ashamed of what he was thinking.

Buck looked at him, "no matter what you think Ben, that man is my grandfather. He cared for me, watched me grow up into a man and was proud of his only grandson. Never once did my mixed blood ever come up. Never once was I looked at as some sort of freak. Never once was I called a savage."

The following day at the appointed time, Buck and Kit drove to the appointed spot and waited for Yellow

Moon to arrive. When the sun was directly overhead, two horses appeared on the ridge and slowly made their way down the ridge. It was Yellow Moon and Spotted Calf, both had war lances, but were held up right now, for battle.

Kit looked at Buck, "Buck?"

"It's alright It's my grandfather, no harm will come to you."

The two came to a stop in front of the wagon and Yellow Moon was the first to speak, "Lone Wolf, it is pleasing to see you and your friend."

Buck looks at Kit, then his grandfather, "Grandfather, this is my friend Katherine Taylor."

The old man notices the look in his grandson's eyes when he looks at the girl, "I am happy you are a friend of Lone Wolf." He looks to his son, "I have heard sad news Lone Wolf. Is it true you have turned your back on your people?"

Buck looks at him, "no Grandfather, I did not. But someone has been making the Paiutes raid the local farmers here and they are raiding the farms, killing the settlers and stealing the cattle."

Yellow Moon looks at his grandson, "and the whites have made the Army attack the Paiutes, were they following your orders?"

"Grandfather, my orders were to come out here and try to stop the fighting and find a peaceful way for the whites and Paiutes to live."

Spotted Calf, who had remained silent all this time could keep still no longer. "Ask him why he lives with this white woman?"

Buck looks at his grandfather, "her father was kind to me when the ranchers beat me and would have killed me if he had not showed up and take me to his house. I owe his family my life."

Spotted Calf looked at Buck, "why does he use a white name? Is it to be like them?"

Buck looks at him then his grandfather, "I use the name of a man I respect as much as my grandfather, my father Buck Cross."

The old man nods and smiles, the boy has showed respect to both men in his life. He has not dishonored his native family, but is trying to find a way that both worlds can live together.
The old man looks at his grandson, "I see you are not trying to destroy us. The stories I have heard are not true." He looked at Spotted Calf, "you knew this, you let me believe Lone Wolf had gone against his people?"

Spotted Calf looked at him, "do not believe him great one. He lies to you now. He lies to save his life and that of the woman."

Yellow Moon looks at Buck, "I believe my grandson and know his heart is where it should be."

"You are an old man who has lost his courage. The great Yellow Moon now sits with the women. No longer does he seek to lead his people."

Yellow Moon looks at him, "I now see who is against their people. You have tried to make it so Lone Wolf is wrong when it is you who are against our people."

He looked at Yellow Moon, "and you are an old man who no longer is worthy of being a chief."

Suddenly Yellow Moon lowered his lance and threw it directly at Spotted Calf. It went through his body and he fell to the ground dead. Yellow Moon looked at Buck. "Spotted Calf will no longer raid your people Lone Wolf, you have my word on this."

"I believe you Grandfather."

The old man looks at Kit, "you have put happiness in my grandson's life and you did not cry out when Spotted Calf fell dead, you are destined to be the one for him."

Kit looks at him, "thank you."

Yellow Moon looks at Buck, "stay well Lone Wolf and when you are whole again come and see your old grandfather sometime."

Buck smiles at him, "I will Grandfather, I promise."

The old man smiles and turns to ride off.

Five years had passed, Buck and Kit had married and Buck was given the position of head of Indian affairs in the territory with a home not far from the border of the Indian land. His job was to maintain peaceful relations with the tribes and the whites as well as keep both sides on their own side.

Yellow Moon had lived to see the path his grandson had taken secure a peaceful existence between whites and the Indians.